Spira

Spiral of Fire

MICHAEL COPE

AFRICASOUTH PAPERBACKS
CAPE TOWN · JOHANNESBURG
DAVID PHILIP

First published 1987 in Africasouth New Writing by David Philip
Publisher (Pty) Ltd, 217 Werdmuller Centre, Claremont,
7700, South Africa

ISBN 0 86486 094 3

Typesetting by Blackshaws (Pty) Ltd. via computer text transfer
Printed by Blackshaws (Pty) Ltd, Cape Town

Contents

I would like to thank everyone who helped with the writing of this book by reading and criticising the manuscript. My special thanks also go to Julia Martin, Jane Taylor, Joan Anderson and all the kind people at Bloublommetjieskloof farm.

For Jack and Lesley, with love

TURNAROUND

When the old servant turns his new face around,
deep fire moving underground.
And when that fire moves into your love:
terror below, thunder above.

*'Ban, 'Ban, Ca-Caliban
Has a new master: get a new man.**

* The last two lines are from *The Tempest* II:ii.

A Crossword Puzzle

9 May 1986

Bam!

The car door closes; he gets into the Golf. The windows
are all steamed up: wipers on, the back one says Groin
Groin. The choke comes out, start nanananananananana-
nanana. Na a a aaa aaaaa. The engine takes, relief. He
revs to let it warm up.

*Let's see, have we got everything? Briefcase, manual, the
other big IDMS one, the diskettes for MicroFocus, keys of
course. Money, fumble in pocket. Money's okay. Check the
tangle of hair in the driving-mirror. Right, let's ... go.*

Billy's on his way to work.

The neat CV misses several important facts, glosses over
other vast ones.

WILLIAM KNOX MARKS
Born in Zambia, November, 1951
Education: Junior school at Sabie Primary, Transvaal
Senior school: Christian Brothers College, Kimberley
University: Wits, Psychology 1: 1969
And so on

Take that entry: Junior school at Sabie Primary. That's
seven years for a helpless little boy with very short blond
curls and freckly snub nose. Seven years of complicated
violence, of Christian National Education, of Meneer van
der Poel and Juffrou Viviers.

Does it say that he writes poetry but never shows it to anyone? You bet it doesn't. Does it say that he suffers from an ulcer, masturbates, was the son of a country doctor, spent a disastrous year at Wits smoking dope and failing everything? It tells you that he's a qualified electrician, that he entered Data Processing in '78 and has worked his way up to a cushy position as a sort of do-all. Programmer/designer/analyst/consultant. But not about the briefcase, about the years with a great fuzzy Afro and bare feet, dodging cops. Six months selling acid, blarneyed himself out of a bust. Curiously, the CV *does* mention, under hobbies and personal interests, the fact that he collects Netsuke.

He has been married once. The marriage ended in late '75 after two and a half hopeless helpless years and he's still paying Cheryl alimony. Her uncle Bernard, mother's brother, handled the divorce for her. Not in the CV.

Does it tell you that he still thinks wild thoughts, rages within himself, riding the acid memories, riding the memories of now-mocked TM, which he spent eighteen months doing? That all his history still lives in him? That his stock response to stress is to fantasise bombing the source, hand-grenade firing-pin still clutched in his teeth? Yet he never went to the army, being a Zambian citizen. The CV will not tell you that he sleeps naked, except for his socks.

His father the doctor, who died in '74 of heart failure, was an old-time Jewish socialist of German extraction (hence the blond hair), for whom the Soviet Union had risen like a bright comet in the twenties and thirties. After the war and Stalin, his faith was slowly sloughed, falling piece by piece from him until he was left bare and without belief, a sneering old man. 'When I was young, I used to say, Up the workers and fuck management. Now I say, Fuck the workers and fuck management.' Dad had spent six months in Spain in 1937, had met Durutti (and disliked him), had met hordes of British volunteers, but never

Orwell or Auden. One day Billy, thirteen and in the middle of reading Anne Frank, had asked Dad about the war, and had used the phrase *holocaust victim*. Dad had looked startled, then stared at him for a long time. Eventually, just before turning away, he'd said: 'Now everyone is a holocaust victim.' Poor old dad, to die a prosperous doctor after all that. Hearing nothing, believing nothing, hoping nothing, enduring.

Billy's on his way to work, injecting himself into traffic's artery; monoxide and mist. The cars are slow this morning, his tweed jacket sways on the jacket hook.

Down Loop Street. Foreshore monolith buildings, the towers of Moloch. The dark cement office block, ease into the covered parking down the spiral, slip the magnetic-strip card into the slot, boom comes up. Roll down three levels under rows of endlessly repeating double fluorescents, leaving the echo of the loose exhaust rumbling.

Elevator up, past the security, flash the card again; no-one really looks.

The corridor's carpeted with beige spicules and soft under his grey moccasins.

— Morning, Caroline.

— Morning, morning. Coffee's on. I can see you need it. Rough night?

He takes in his reflection in the grey glass panel.

Hair's standing up at the back again. Shit. Pat it down saying:

— No, average actually. I went to bed early, slept like a buffalo. How long're you going to be on the word-processor?

Caroline is immaculate, some mannikin from a fashion store window.

Christ, she must be wearing a pound of make-up again. How does she use the keyboard with those nails?

She flicks the long flop of modish fringe out of her eyelashes, shuffles a file of papers.

— As soon as I've done these letters you can have it.

— Thanks, sweet of you.

Head for the office kitchen. The filter machine's giving a death rattle, nearly done. Pour coffee, light a cig. On to the office cubicle, still carrying the manuals. Nip into Raj's stall and rip off his paper, he'll know where to find it.

He sits down at his desk, drops the pile of stuff, spreads the paper.

Crossroads, KTC, unrest report: page 2. The death toll's up somewhere in the eighties and climbing, that's official. Since when? The war burns nearer, the third-world war. Turn to the comics, quickly. Oh, dearie me! Eve Jones has broken her leg. Crossword. Don't look at the leader. Crossword's wonderful for that, making its own little world of crazy word logic. Hmm ... Tao poets' food (8) ... easy, potatoes.

— Morning, Bill. At it again?

— Ja. I can't get three across. *That is the question whether (1,1,2).*

— Let's see? Oh, you've just started. *That is the question whether.* Dumb clue. The first part must be I E. Gimme a quick look at the front page. What's the Rand at? Thirty-two forty-five. Shit. Gold's up though. Look at this: Lieutenant Laubscher of the SAP denied last night that the police have taken sides in the black-on-black violence at Crossroads squatter camp.

— Never believe anything till it's been officially denied.

— By the way, what are you working on these days?

— Same. The specs for the big creditors' system interface. Boring's hardly the word.

— Not doing any overtime?

— I might have to. The whole thing's getting bogged down. I mean look at the size of this. You can't keep all of it in your mind at the same time. It's a job for a team, not one guy. And the designs for the existing system are hopeless as well as outdated. Raj's trying to fill me in on all the informal changes but it's hopeless. Aagh, I'll just plod on and try to come in within a week or two of the deadline.

— Ow. Sorry I asked. But listen, I may just have a bit of moonlighting for you if you're interested. I was going to do it myself, but a couple of other things have come up.

— I'll definitely think about it. When's it for?

— Oh, maybe starting next week some time, a bunch of evenings. The pay seems bloody good. It's heavy-duty security stuff by the sound of it, on IBM kit. You should be able to eat it up. I don't have all the details.

— Thanks, Dave. I'll let you know by Friday.

— Well, I tell you what. I'll pop the guy's name and phone number on your desk some time today. If you haven't come back to me by Friday I'll phone him myself and say it's off.

The guy's name is van Wijk. Ensel van Wijk. From a firm called Crencor, of which he's never heard.

Hell, are there really van Wyks that spell their names like that, with an IJ?

— Thank you for calling Crencor good morning, *goeie more*.... I'm reengeeng.... He's not at his desk, please hold while I page him. Thank you.

Computerised version of Campdown Races ... doo daa, doo daa....

— Still no reply, but he's definitely in the building.... No sir, I'm sorry that's jus how the exchange ees. There's no way I can turn it off. There's a lot of people that asks for it off....

Campdown racetrack five miles long, doo daa do

— I found him, you going through.

— Van Wijk.

— Morning Mister van Wijk. Bill Marks here from Datlin. That's Marks as in Marks and Spencer. Dave Mac-Farlaine asked me to contact you.

— Oh, yes, MacFarlaine. Ja.

— He said he'd phone you.

— No, I haven't received any call from him.

— Oh. Well, he said he would, and he suggested that I may be able to stand in for him. You know, do the work. Something else has come up for him, see, which means he won't be able to do it. And I'd be available. Dave and I, we work together here at Datlin, doing more or less the same job. Same machines anyway.

— Well, I'll have to wait for his personal confirmation of this. Can I get your number there?

— I'll get the call transferred to him right now if that's all right with you.

— No, fine.

— Dave, I've got your van Wijk chap on the line. He wants you to tell him that I'm the man for the job. Who the hell is he anyway?

— Put him through, I'll talk later.

A long silence as Billy shuffles through the specifications he's drawing up.

Reach for the phone. No, wait. But the vision of an exhausting and time-consuming job to fill the gap's helluva appealing.

— Hello, Mister van Wijk. Marks here again. I seem to have lost your call after Dave got it.

— No trouble Mister Marks. Could you come in at say, one fifteen on the sixteenth, that's a Friday, and we'll have a little chat and then hopefully we can wrap something up.

— Let me have a quick look in the old diary. Sure. One fifteen on the nail. Look forward to meeting you.

— Thank you Mister Marks, bye.

— Bye.

Coffee, back to the crossword. Seven across.... Beginning to be or not to be? (4) with an S in the second place. Hn.... Put it away, put it away. Let's see now.... Control file flags. The operating system should do all this. What exactly is FPIND? Ah, here. After the matching-record, before the next, turn it on, turn it off again here. That would make, er, up to twelve thousand extra reads and writes. Must be a more elegant way of doing it. Bugger elegance. And pick it up here. Pseudo-COBOL.

```
IF FPIND EQ '/*'
   AND SEQUENCE_NUMBER LT LAST_
      RECORD_READ
         AND IF EOFIND EQ 'ON'
            THEN MOVE 'COMPLETE' TO SUCCESS
               PERFORM CLOSE_FILES_ROUTINE
            ELSE IF EOFIND NE 'ON'
            MOVE 'PARTIAL' TO SUCCESS
            MOVE LAST_RECORD_READ TO WLAST
            PERFORM CANCEL_UPDATE_ROUTINE
ENDIF.
```

Citadel

9 May 1986

The car stops, engine giving its extended pre-ignition shudder even after it's turned off. Out of the car, jingling keys. Clutching two shopping-bags and the briefcase under the arm. Gate opens kreeenk. Nudge letterbox lid up with briefcase hand, peer in. Same junk from yesterday. Up the path, unlock, open.

There are familiar smells: the recent varnish on the floor, stale Gitane smoke. He dumps the carrybags on the kitchen counter, throws the briefcase at the settee, heads for the lavatory.

That's Karma. Come home with a normal run-of-the-mill bladder and no sooner is the front door closed than the piss-trigger is flipped. Gotto go, even if there's only a few drops. It comes from those times risking stop streets and traffic lights with a burster, jiggling bumcheeks to keep it in. Dash for the porcelain, ah, bliss is release. But leaving the imprinted pattern, a lurking bladder ghost somewhere in the passage.

In the kitchen, he packs the groceries away: cheese in its little compartment in the fridge door, milk below it, rice into the big ball-jar. The packet is folded and put into the bottom drawer. Surfaces are wiped with one of those plastic pseudo-cloths. Back in the sitting-room, he moves the briefcase to stand against the wall by the door.

Sit down. Breathe out. What now?

Wrong. Wrong-ong-ong. Shouldn't have asked it, can't unask it. What indeed, to pass the time, in this beautiful paid-

up aesthetic house? Patrimony, the fatted calf.... You're filling time, Bill. Scuffle for the kitchen.

It's a hollow feeling bumbling in the head, that feeling from when he was little, of rubbery gungey something just off the sides of the field of vision, of dead tingling in the limbs, what to do next? The diary's empty for once. No-one has phoned. The house is tidy. Cynthia's been, leaving two neat heaps of ironing on the foot of the bed to make a dent in the black duvet cover. He feels her efforts to be almost intrusive on his habitual tidiness.

First line of defence: Consume. Go for the fridge. Liquifruit Pear. Open it with the kitchen shears. Glug Glug into the glass. Yaah too thick and sweet. Dilute with last night's dry white. Pace. Drink. Look for something to tidy. The shears. The little cardboard offcut from the carton. Wipe the table. Again the question: what now. Too early for supper. Don't want to eat out again. The telly. Fuck the telly.

Upstairs to the bedroom. The irresistible cupboard, look somewhere else.

There's a neat stack of books by the bed: seven books, four of them science fiction. He stands and stares at the pile of books until they're no longer books but a series of bright lines of colour. Blue Pelican, rich red hardcover: minimalist stripes. The table becomes a set of funny angles in white. He turns without knowing it ... back down to the sitting-room.

Flop in a chair. Close eyes, breathe, what now?

What happened at work to freak me out? Pretty ordinary day, the usual pressures, Rick full of shit again about the spec, but he's always going on about something. He needs it, it's like water to a fish. Crencor or whatever stuff no problem. Dave reckons something like two grand for a week's work. Nice one. No, nothing I couldn't handle, at least I think not, nothing ...

... Breathe ...

... it's the bloody situation, so hard to take things seriously

when everywhere else the seriousness is of such a different order. Requirements definition for the creditors' system interface. *Fuck. Under that smoke out there, tired hungry people, real flesh and bloody meat people, waiting for the rain to come. Waiting to make a connection. Waiting for a cousin, an uncle, aunt. Waiting for the Casspir to rattle past. Waiting in the wind, waiting in foodlines, lines for cast-off clothes from Rondebosch and Newlands. Wonder what the roadblocks are like tonight?...*

Time for the Anarchists, for them to act. For the crazy individualists, the wild communards. And what would my lady in the book say about all this?

Something moves up on him from the shadow-place down there. But it's not a jolting kick, rather a long slow rubbery sinking-in, a subtle adjustment of attitude. Mapped, this intuition might show the restless barbarian hordes massed to the north, leather-clad chieftains, camps being broken, dirty-blue plumes from early fires. Horsemen geared up in the dawn, weapons rattling. To the south, the smooth plains below the passes. The innocent and cruel empire slumbers with cities, the glow of villages, farmers and farmers' wives, cattle driven in to be milked. But now the book, a defending wall, springs up: slicing the map in two, and the empire becomes a defended citadel of waking consciousness.

The book, I'll look at the book again.

Light a smoke, up the stairs again, to the spare-room/study. Now, where is it? In the bottom desk-drawer, at the back, corrugated cardboard filing-box. Notes, notes. Hardly a completed passage. Here's the oracle, the divination system of the bronze plates and the axle. All sketches and plans.

Christ, a whole system of its own here, and I can remember hardly a thing about how it works, what the funny little glyphs mean. And all done in sepia ink! When did I have a sepia pen? Must have been that Rotring, ja, looks like Rotring. And here's the part where he's travelling.

*I am at a crossroad in the middle of the southern flat-
lands, heading south-east to find them. The plain runs un-
dulatingly in all directions. There is a ruin near the road,
an old stone structure, sand blown up against the gap-
tooth wall, with little grey-green weeds poking from among
the cracks. I climb onto a big rock to get a better view.
From up here it's no different. Long hills like petrified
dunes, with big roundish boulders tumbled onto them,
seemingly at random. I try to explain to myself how the
stones got there, but my knowlege of geophysical things is
so meagre as to leave me imagining huge hands scattering
them like marbles. The real story must be much more interesting. A saga of glaciers, vast pressures, sudden faults,
and ancient erosion; slow, patient and indifferent. In
among the rocks stand the unbelievable trees, huger than
the few Sequoia left on earth. They are widely spaced;
there are probably a hundred or so of them, if I look all
round. They seem alien, both to me and to the environment. Perhaps they were planted. The area is barren, dry.
The trees must dig deep for water, rooting down to bed-
rock. There are no farmsteads here. There is nothing but
the scrubby hills, the stones and the trees.*

*I can see the three people who travelled with me, two
women and a teenage boy. And when we arrived, two old
folk were already here, squatting in the shade near the
ruin, shoulders touching. For a long time they did nothing
but look towards the south-east. I approached them and
tried to start a conversation.*

*'Where have you come from?' They both stared at me,
and one pointed down the southern road.*

*'Ah, that's where I'm heading. I'm waiting for the truck
through.'*

'So are we.'

'Oh. I thought you said you'd just come from there.'

*'We were born there. We are sister and brother. You
are not from the south. You sound like someone who has*

learned our language without speaking it.' A long silence.

'This is true. I have arrived recently.'

'You are not a northerner.' She said the word as though its meaning were more than geographical, but I couldn't grasp the particular nuance.

'No. I come from another world,' I offer, expecting surprise.

'Ah, you have come through the spheres then. Which world do you come from?'

'The world is called Earth,' I said, pointing at the sky. The man shut his eyes for about half a minute. Then he said, 'Your world is in that direction,' indicating a spot downwards and to his left. They both closed their eyes. Lying on a fallen slab from the ruin was a bundle tied in blue cloth, faded but clean. It must have contained their possessions. I walked back to my vantage-point.

The old couple seem to be playing a game in the dust, drawing and crossing out lines with a stick. The game is accompanied by a constant patter, but the words are lost in the wind. The other three share food. Suddenly, by the ruin, the game has stopped: the woman starts dancing on her haunches, singing. The others don't even look up. I am overcome with an unimaginable sensation of foreignness and longing, sitting on my rock with the dust and the trees.

Hmm. Some of this is quite interesting, but bits are crap and, God, some of those stubby sentences'll have to be smoothed over, for sure though. Ern, I think the tense is jumping about. Wonder how that'll read?

Howsabout I have had enormous difficulty translating from their language into ours, not only because the culture is almost totally alien, in the most literal sense, but because the language is being changed and used as a philosophic tool. Where new meanings have been created, or in instances where there simply is no appropriate English word, I have had to try using such approximations as I could find as well as *cobbling together terms of my own. This, along with my own admittedly clumsy style, has tended to give an unnecessarily formal tone, where no formality originally existed. Even though I did a thorough theoretical study of the language and was assisted in the field and later during the writing of this by sophisticated and fairly up-to-date translation software, I was often unable to follow things that were said, and have had to piece several passages together by inference, intuition and guesswork.*

Unh, that bit reads like a publisher's disclaimer or something. I'm really going to have to change the narrative to let it live less in his defences and get more into his head. Boring. And, funny, I don't remember writing any of it. Not the actual typewriter-pounding.... I was often unable to follow things that were said, and have had to piece several passages together by ... I can't feel it. This is the old Remington, which means '79 or before. Unbelievable.

By now pages are being spread on the carpet in heaps.

Poems mixed in, here's one from Maseru, shouldn't be here. I'll file it later.

FAT CLOUDS

Fat clouds flying north
Heading for the Summerland
(Winter coming after them
With a cold hand).

Last night I saw the Summer's queen
Lying face-down in the mud.
Saddened, but not crying, she
Had foreign matter in her blood.

All of Europe's blood in me
Twisted with a pulling wrench.
Lying on the red earth she
Speaks beautiful accented French.

Inside, last night, the dancing still
Goes on, the music still goes round.
The people from the Summerland
Pretend it's still a tourist town.

She's made of flesh and piano-wire,
Carmine varnish for her mouth.
Above us the night clouds fly
From the 'Switzerland of the South'.

Images of Africa,
Metaphors of sweat and hate
(But softened by retreating clouds)
Wait for her just beyond the gate.

*God, Maseru! Feels like just the other day, and how long
ago like things getting smaller down a road. Poor Jeanne all
beautiful and so thin and drunk, put it in the pile over there.
These are notes, only. The system for inventing alien words
without really trying: Nice one Squire. Swap most of the
vowels and consonants around. V becomes B, D is T, Ch is
Th ... and then pull the word from English or Afrikaans and
pump it through, hnn, I could write a little program to do it in
about five minutes.*

And the briefcase in the bedroom wardrobe, and the
barbarian hordes massing on the passes, the soldiers
gunned down and the children burned in their homes, the
farm labourers and the exiles, policemen's wives in policemen's houses ... go. Things start to disappear and slip
away: the restless feelings, the holes in the news, the intuition of a networked world out there from which this
house, this particular life, locks him out — all become invisible. The passion of the book is revived; a new world
where he has mastery. He moves to take possession of his
citadel.

Outside a woman's voice shouts high and real. A truck
grates on Mill Street.

Fibres

5 June 1986

He's sitting in the big chair, coffee mug making a ring on the teak arm. It's a Morris chair, made by an uncle in the twenties. There are cushions and a handwoven carpet from the Ciskei. His fingers work slowly into the muscles of her shoulders, untangling the fine organic threads, helping them to flow and slide over each other. A touch with tension in it holds back, stiffens the fingers and pulls the palm up. Rather, the hand should feel down through the whole soft palm, through the warm skin and down into the muscles; it's as though he can feel inside under the skin to the slime-and-blood interior of her.

Catch those slight swellings around the base of the skull, her hair rubbing with the softest crackle in the grooves of fingerprints.

He takes a sip of coffee, and his hands are warmed on the mug. The record is going click-whoosh, click-woosh, faintly in the background, being ignored.

— Ow, yes, there mmm, but not so hard, unh ...

— She's teaching me. She keeps trying to tell me things, you know, I suppose things that have always been in me, but which I'm not really aware of ...

— That's crap, Bill. Are you trying to tell me she's a ghost or something? That she's apart from you, out there?

— Ectoplasm.... No, of course, but that's not what I mean.... She has the air of a real person about her though, an independent entity of some sort. She comes out with phrases and things that I'd never have thought up. Consciously. I can have dialogues with her.

Sue puts on her best mock-psychologist accent:

— Now just relax and tell me. 'Do you hear voices?' Ow, ow ... not so hard....

— Sorry, I didn't hear that.

— Billy, but you must realise that it is all you. Everything. You already know it. Dreams are you, personalities in your head are you. Your characters in the book, they're you also. Should they be someone else already?

— No, doctor. Yes doctor madam sir. Now I feel much more individuated. I accept responsibility for all my selves. I'm not alone any more. Yay, wheee! How's this feel here under here?

— Jesus, softly kiddo. Are you trying to tear my arm off?

Fingers in there under the shoulderblade, stretching that rubbery skin up, probing for tensions, tendons ... move and relax, sway the arm gently to lift here, ah.

— Ah, now the other one, relax the arm, don't fight it.

Slowly, breathing rhythms start to change. He's sitting forward, she's crosslegged, upright between his knees, jersey pulled askew as his hands work the plump little layers of protection around each vertebra, thumbs smooth into the valleys between. Long muscles have hardened with holding posture, tensing as if for the blow that still hasn't landed.

Click-whoosh, click-whoosh, click-whoosh....

— Can I talk to her too? I mean, could I ask her a question?

— Why not lie on the futon and cover up with a blanket. A question? ... I don't know. I told you, I don't even have a name for her yet. I think she's a complex, a sort of lens. Yes, like that. Just let the small of your back peep out. I'm still looking for her name. Come on, you could help me.

There are whorls of tiny hairs on whitest skin. He rubs the oil in, following their pattern, tracing the direction, hard and harder along the mirrored spirals, in to where dimples may have been, feels the top of hipbone with thumbs and moves up along the edges of the spine bump bump bump....

She says:

— Well, it's got to have *ma* in it: the primal mother sound.

— All right, Ma what? Mah-jong? Mahound? Maher. That's an okay-sounding one. Maher.

— Ungh, gimme a sip. Maher. But pronounced Mahair.

— Mmm, it's interesting, I'll hang on to it for the mean-while. Still a bit reminiscent of Mahler or Meher Baba ...

— Or Mother, for that matter. Ow, eina! Careful.

— Sorry. Ja, maybe we ditch the Ma idea.... I also don't want it to sound too Indian, Mahawhatever, or Karma, Dharma, Rama, Padmasambhava ...

— Blahma Wanagada malafablah. Why not just call her mommy and be done?

— Because she's *not* mommy, that's why. Mommy's something else, the archetypes hardly even seem to overlap. Is it sore here?

— Not really. The neck was the worst, but I think it's made a difference already. Ooh, yes. That's ouch. Thhh. No, no. You can go hard.... What about Mylia?

— Mylia? Where'd you get that from? Is it a name?

— No, I made it up. It is a name now, though. Don't you think it sounds good? Mylia, Myleea ...

— I like it. Hang on, I'll write it down. In case I forget. How do you spell it? Em why el eye ay. Right. Thanks. Where was I?

... Lower back, upper spine, skin glowing flushed red as the arteries open, all that blood and warmth flooding in to relax the long string muscle fibres, mmm.

— Ask her a question for me.

— This isn't a séance. As you were at pains to tell me. But if you ask me a question, I'll try to tell you what she might say.

— Okay, ask her, 'What is evil?'

— Jeez, well there we go! Given the mere *finger* of an offer to play with my fantasy, she tears off, hell, more than an *arm*. You never were one to settle for the small things, were you? Who the hell do you think I am, Dostoievski? I should tell you that the answer is forty-two.

— Or six-six-six. Ask her anyway.

— Okay, here goes. But any resemblance to persons living or dead is purely occidental.

Eyes closed, call to her. She's sitting on the wide veranda outside the communal kitchen. Easy, squatting in the sun with several others. It's late afternoon.

Someone (is it a man?) is breast-feeding a child. Shouts and squeals from farther out; children are playing a game. They're not just kids but adults too and there's a lot of running and touching. The game seems rough and gentle at the same time. I come and stand near her. Mylia. She and another are looking at some sort of mechanical device.

'See, it's worn down here,' holding it up to the light. 'You could spit through the gap where the shaft runs.'

The man with her sees me, pats the ground next to him. 'A brass sleeve around here ought to keep it running until Annar gets a chance to turn up a new one.' I sit down next to them.

— Well, what does she say?

— Gimme a chance. I've only just sat down next to her. She's busy examining a part of some machine. Looks like a worn pump. I think Mylia is a good name for her.

She holds the broken part and jiggles the axle. Toc toc. 'If we put a bearing here, there'll be no need for a new one, and the wear ought to be reduced. See, the bearing here, in a turned groove so wide, and a little oilgate here that expands with heat to let just so much oil through.

We'll go up to the workshop with Annar tonight.' She hands me the part. I hold it on my crosslegged lap and look at it. It's incomprehensible, made of a fairly light whitish metal, and has no feeling of familiarity about it. A little oil oozes out onto my trousers. I look at her.

'Peter.' She has the usual mispronunciation but there's a humour in her look. 'You want to ask me a question.'

'I want to ask you millions of questions.'

'What gave you the idea that I would be a good person to come to for the asking of questions? We all have similar ideas. Any one of us could talk to you.'

'You're the — how should I say? — the person of power, here. That's why I come to you.'

She laughs gently, in her throat. A fifty-year-old worker's throat with wrinkles, the tendons and veins showing.

'That's the language of the north. Everyone here has power, which means that no-one has it. What do you want to ask me?'

'It's difficult. Now I feel as if this isn't the time to ask such a question.'

I am acutely aware of everything that's around me. I hear the sound of scrubbing coming from inside the building behind us and the people playing in the courtyard. The character of the tiles we sit on, cracked and worn, a pale amber colour, with dust motes picking up the golden sunlight seems both important and ordinary. People are re-laxing after a day's work, talking. Someone has a big leaf that holds a pile of little round sweetmeats. There are the first sunset tinges on the clouds to the north, and the eastern hillside reaches up with its dusk shadowline.

'Well, I wanted to ask you ... What is evil?'

'And?'

'And, well yes ...' Her eyes engage mine fully. Her at-tention is a strange, almost tangible thing. 'That's my ques-tion.'

'I'm not sure I follow. Surely the word has a meaning for you?'

'Of course. It's just that, er ... I don't know what that meaning is any more. My thoughts have been disturbed since I came here.'

'You've forgotten?

'Yes, yes I think so.... No, I do know what it means, but this meaning also seems to have got all twisted up. I was really asking you what your meaning for the word is.'

'Oh, well that's easy. The people here say that evil is co-ercion.'

Her answer catches me off-guard. I look down at the dusty surface of the tiles. After a long time, I say: 'Thank you. I'm not sure that the people where I come from would say that. Certainly some say the opposite, that evil is stepping out of line, is not being coerced.'

— She told me. It seems so bloody simple. I refuse to believe that I came up with that answer all of my own. Sly old woman.

— What did she say?

— She said, 'The people here say that evil is coercion.' So there's your arm and a half.

— Hey! That's a fine one. I like it. Billy, you're a sly old woman. Did she get her pump fixed?

— Read the book and find out. Though I don't think the pump'll be in the book. But d'you see what I mean? She is teaching me. It's hard to believe that sort of com-pactness, simplicity, comes from the me that I know so well. And I really have to conjure her up. Set and setting, the whole thing.

— You seemed to take ages about it. Do you see her? A visual image?

— It's hard to say. Not really a picture before the eyes, though I do know what things look like, in the sense that I could easily describe them. But it's more like telling a story, or remembering something. There really aren't

words for it. 'Imagination' has been buggered up so as to
mean any old thing.... You just sort of know what you're
describing.

— What does she look like?

— Hmm, that's an example. No actual picture springs to
mind, but I *am* clear about what she's like. Tall, taller
than you. About five eleven or so. Fiftyish. Short manage-
able hair, steel grey. But not mannish, not cropped. Just
ordinary short grey hair, about up to here. Darkish skin.
Like we'd think of a North Indian or a Malay. Very high
hooked nose, a bit like Edith Sitwell. With full, almost ne-
groid lips. Strong but not square jaw. An oval face, surrounded by a frost of hair. She's physically powerful, from
lots of agricultural work, besides being big. And she's
always doing something, ploughing, composting, fixing a
wall. Golden eyes. Not pale-brown, but an almost metallic
golden. Her skin's getting old now, she's got a few
wrinkles, especially around her eyes, and the skin on her
neck's a bit loose. Oh, and her eyebrows and lashes are
still black.

— And her name's Mylia. I hope I'll get a credit for
that.

— Surely and all. In the dedication at the front. For
Sue, who named Mylia. It is a good name for her. With
my love. You'll want to do a few spine stretches now to
get your back really loose.

— Yes, doctor. Tell me the worst, doctor, will I pull
through?

— Nasty vengeful girl!

— Just as nasty as Billy the Pig.

— Oink oink.

The Picture

27 October 1972 (remembered)

It was October, late in the month. Spring, Namaqualand daisies in full bloom, fields of them, whole real three-dee postcards of them stretching as far as... And in Cape Town here, one of those immaculate warm spring evenings when you go bounce-walking on rubbersoles, along the beachfront just to watch the old men seriously exchanging latest news about their hearts or businesses. Kugels. Blue-rinse matrons with almost-pink poodles, a higher chatter of conversation. Domestic workers in uniforms, or perhaps changed into a mini for strolling, transistor radio with Engelbert Humperdinck, Tom Jones Why why why Delilah? Doodn doodn doodn dooo. The Beatles now unbanned, Donovan and all other unremembered songs. Beachfront. Under the boardwalk.

Later a pizza or calamari — little assholes in batter — eaten outdoors under canvas awning gazing into the sunset street, carlights coming on in the semi-dark. Discreet Indian waiters turn a blind eye to Aatjie's skin, making nothing of the clandestine illegalities. Walk again and on to retsina slipped under the counter in a Greek café with all the vibratos and hey, that's weird, this one sounds suspiciously akin to an Irish jig! The tired old wife of the café-owner wears black with a white apron. Someone has died, maybe Jesus. The plastic flowers have greasy kitchen dust and there's a fishing-net on the ceiling. Vine-leaves stuffed with rice and something that tastes like capers and as the retsina

seeps in and the evening possesses you, everything is suf-
fused with that 1972 air of irreality.

   The year! Long-haired boys and dope, and the fading of
the hip time, if the signs could be read. Conspiracies, the
music, guitars (electric, naturally), the crash-pads with all
those weird out-of-town strangers sleeping in the broken
empty rooms of recently vacated group-area houses.... Sleep
here, shit here, bust pipes here, fuck here. Four corners of a
room and a view from the rooftops out onto Table Bay and
Robben Island and the tankers oozing Arab oil and the
sharks and dolphins and snoek, on forever beyond ... the
sea. Make a fire in the middle of the floor till it burns the
boards, then move into the back room upstairs. The one
with the pictures that someone did while tripping. Swirling
lines trying to trace the fade-and-run patterns of the halluci-
nation. A single word in dripping aluminium paint:
   APRICOT
I'm strolling in the thick of the warm spring air with Cheryl
and Aatjie/Fuad, high as kites on these little red pills; some
kind of speed, maybe, or is it for asthma or heart condi-
tions? ... whatever. Car-noise going Wabba-dabba dabbada
a-da-da-da, the brights catching us full-face as they come
around the corner up near the traffic lights. Robots. Jesus,
robots! Metal pole-stripe men from the sci-fi horror world
of the future all disguised as harmless lights, now you stop,
now you go nowYOUstop NOWyouGO amber now, easy.
... flash red. ... flash green. ... flash amber, hmm ... maybe
the official answer to all that privately owned neon. Only,
the state can use the law, backed by the traffic police,
straight police, paramilitary, etc., etc., to enforce obedience.
The rest have to use subtler persuasions.

   — Shit, Aatjie, get the picture — *and the picture is a*
tangible big boiling thing *which can be got* — if the ordinary owner of a neon-sign could force you to obey the
signs — Hey, buddy — *fake American accent* — I see you
aren't buying Coke right now. What's this shit you're

drinking? I see. Brand X? Well, didn't you read the sign
back there? It said clearly THINGS GO BETTER WITH
COKE. That'll be twenty bucks for ignoring the lights and,
let's see now, another thirty for reckless consuming....

— What you talking about?

— Traffic lights. Robots.

— Coca Cola?

— Forget it

Wabba-dabba-dabadadda-dabada-da-da-da-da

*In those days one — well, this one anyway — was politically
naive. Very. One hadn't heard of Soweto Day or Mayday,
Plutonium, National Forum, UDF, all those beautiful community organisations, nothing. Which is to say something else,
which is to say things were different, different enough to make
you blind if you were white and all right. Sure, Sharpeville,
but that was years ago. Sure the ANC and PAC were somewhere out there. And the revolution would come and Mandela would stride like Adamastor in from Robben Island.
Remember 'And the Seagull's name was Nelson, Nelson who
came from the sea'?*

There was a buddy of Billy's who had this idea: he was
going to swim to the Island because he'd sussed out the
connection between the Great White Mandala and the
Great Black Mandela, and he just had to get there, a sort
of aquatic pilgrimage. Billy's mind filled with an image of
Jake flinging his stoned immaculate pale pink body into
the Atlantic, limbs flailing in a frenzy of speed, until he
should flounder among seals and snoek, the crabs
wreathing his hair. These are pearls....

He'd had to spend hours talking him out of it. Well, not
so much talking as signalling, trading in the currency of
common symbols. Like playing bits of records:

    And the cloud looked down
    upon the lake.
    And saw his detachedness
    from a former face ...

And saw his changingness and cried aloud ...
To be a double for the sky.
Shuffling photos of Macartney and Jim Morrison into the Tarot deck.... In the end he stayed and they rolled a joint up on the roof. Seagulls wheeling about an old woman's bread.

Billy was in a protest that year, at Saint George's Cathedral....
You know — Hey, those bastards are at it again. The State, Authority.
— What was it that time? Twenty-two detainees? or what? Was that the time before? Memory goes all fuzzy over the intervening years. No, come on, it's not that bad but I never was a NUSAS heavy, wasn't really *in* on the thing: rather, a loose electron buzzing on the excitement, the feeling that here was something happening, that, well, you know ... no sense of history. And there I was painting these posters for them to hold up. The boys in wide bell-bottoms, styled after Mick Jagger or Danny Le Rouge, girls with pale Mary Quant faces and that hairstyle that comes to two points along the jawline, like this. Painting VORSTER NAZI, JUSTICE FOR ALL and so on. The guys across the street such Dick-Tracey obvious fuzz in their raincoats with great erect zoom lenses, snap whizz, snap whizz. Hell, there must be a file that thick on me somewhere. And then the Kolonel over the road goes squawk squawk on his megaphone in both official languages, indecipherable in either, and they're charging. Did they have dogs there may have been dogs I don't remember ... but I do remember a great big black truncheon swinging from that little string which goes around the wrist and I do remember the face of one of them grinning, I was in the third rank from the front. With Kosie just in front of me.
— Did I ever tell you about Kosie? Crazy bugger from

Springs or Brakpan, or somewhere on the outer reaches of the Reef. Surname Bezuidenhoudt. He was with us in the workshop and came along to the cathedral for the fun. Not a political thought in his head, but he hated cops, you know, poor and endlessly stuffed around. Anyway, the heavies come jogging over to Saint George's…. Wow, think of that, Saint Bloody George the wormslayer presiding over the whole event! Have you ever been baton-charged? No, of course not. It gave me some inkling of what it may be like to be raped. I was teargassed in '76 in the middle of Town and sat in the Scotch Coffee House watching through a locked glass door as two great camou-flaged thugs cornered a black girl in school uniform. She couldn't have been more than twelve or thirteen. No shit. Right there in front of me, on the other side of the plate-glass, they laid into her something terrible…. Doef doef doef. They were enjoying it, you could see. She screamed a lot and there was blood. You can take it from me, I felt totally helpless and just let myself cry, pretending that it was the gas.

— Oh, yes…. Here I am in the third row and they come charging over the road and before you can say John Vorster the front row have got it and the crowd is starting to behave exactly like a panicking crowd. Gone all thoughts of peaceful defiance or whatever, all they want to do is get the hell back into the cool interior of the cath-edral. I just pick up my feet and let their pressure carry me up the steps towards the doors. And right there in front of me is Kosie, not struggling with us to get inside but leaning onto me and the rest of the solid mass of us for a purchase, so that he can take a roadhouse kick into the face of the first cop to come within footreach. I could see the whole action as if in slow motion. All my internal organs curdled and I was ready to kiss him goodbye. I started pulling on his collar. Can you *imagine* what would have *happened* to him? And the rest of us, by association?

So, right at the crucial moment, microseconds before he could get his big Benoni foot in, the charge is called off. All the kids kept right on squeezing into the doorway. Those were the days when people still had quaint notions like the sanctity and inviolability of the Church. Was that '71 or '72? My memory really does go all odd and, let me tell you, I am totally ashamed to confess that I don't remember which particular atrocity the whole thing was about. 'Twenty-two detainees' is the phrase that sticks in my mind, so I'll hang my hat on it, but don't make me swear.

One was naive, sure, but barreling along the boulevard, the smell of kelp and sea oozing in from the Atlantic as the cold air shifted, it's a really exceptional spring night. Me and Aatjie piling into the front of the Kombi, Cheryl battling to slide the big sand-clogged door open, in at the side, close it slam. Sink into foam plastic, breathe out like the foam. The sound comes on, Jethro Tull:

  I cease to see where I'm goin'
  I cease to see where I'm goin' ...
  I dont want to!

Cape Town nightstreets. Aatjie driving, king of caution, both hands clutching the wheel till the veins stand out.

To Vaughn's place, or rather to Jessica-and-Vaughn's place. New Church Street, an old Victorian double-story with all the vestiges of colonial splendour, of the invisible servants cloistered in attic or basement waiting for the master's command. Upstairs is a library with shelves behind glass doors, now holding only books on concept art, avant-garde sculpture, absurdist theatre, a whole huge Science Fiction collection, Ken Kesey, Tim Leary, Malraux and Marcuse, Marx and Gramsci. Brecht. Agehananda Bharati, Krishnamurti, Charan Singh, Paramhansa Yogananda. Service bells in every room, miraculously still working with a big old doubledecker battery, causing an imperious buzzing in the kitchen and a little flap clicks back revealing the summoning room-number.

There's hardly any furniture, but a litter of Vaughn's sculptures fills all available spaces: a huge stainless-steel bowl filled with watermelon rinds and sinking casts of clenched fists, now covered with a rich velvety grey mold. Life-masks of everyone, with blood-red paint or peace-in-the-home spewing from eyes, nose, mouth. The kitchen's a local disaster area. Wipe as you need or eat from the can.

And in the middle of it all, Jessica, the cyclone's eye, earning the rent, being the grown-up, always calm and clear and precise with her long red hair, with her pale milk skin, looking down at you always though she may not have been taller. Our housemother. God, we looked at her so tenderly with big belladonna drug eyes. Jess. Why?

— It's hard to talk about Jess after all that. Though I really suppose she was some kind of a creature of her time, of the age. That sounds like bullshit. It is bullshit. I don't know. I ask myself that question often. Yes, even these days. What's it now, fourteen years later? Something like that. You know, as I spoke then, you know, when I said 'That question, I ask myself that question,' I couldn't think what the question was. She ... well, her presence there in that place, the house, her presence provokes a huge feeling of question inside me. Why didn't she just, uh, walk away, walk away from it all? You know? I really thought she was free enough to make those kind of choices and I... Aah, fuck it. Actually I didn't think anything of the sort. Don't let me bullshit you; I didn't think about it, not at all. About her when she was there. You know, we just weren't into *thinking*.

— ... Yes, I know what you mean. She did seem older than us. She was older, more mature, less what? Stupid? Now I'm apologising. She was actually fucked. She seemed so big and strong and she was totally fucked all the time and we were too stupid to see it. And sometimes I think that what fucked her up was us, was our love and dependence and, well, you know the story. And maybe *she* was

in love with an idea that just never materialised. Reality
and her vision just got farther and farther apart. I suppose
we all thought she was in love with Vaughn too. Aah,
shit.

... *Jessica and Vaughn and Nick and anyone who might be
passing through and need a couch or piece of floor. And
Arnold, though he preferred to be called 'just Arn', presum-
ably after the Prince Valiant offspring. Arnold the brooding
hermit, the Mystic Prince, quietly working on Hitler's horo-
scope or ploughing through the Egyptian Book of the Dead or
something. And charming those schoolgirls into his spermy
sleeping-bag, one candle and three sticks of incense burning as
the soft bodies roll in the damp mysterious night.*

*Oh, well, bump bump bump up the funny stairs to his
room.*

And at the moment Billy and Cheryl enter, Rachel
comes naked from the bathroom, towel casually over one
shoulder, water puddling around her feet, her wonderful
long toes like a Botticelli, and dries herself conspicuously
in front of the wardrobe mirror.

They sit down, Billy looking too hard in every other direction. Cheryl, crosslegged, goes for a book. Billy says

— Tell me something about Aquarians.

— Are you one?

No reply.

— Aquarians are ... perverted.

— Hey, c'mon. You mean perverse.

— Perverted.

Five minutes pass in silence while Rachel dresses,
choosing a black Israeli robe with fine-point embroidery
yoke, combing out the long dark hair so that the drops
rattle on the grass matting. Arn sits laboriously cleaning,
filling and lighting his crooked pipe. The smell of good
Latakia tobacco fills the room. It comes from mainland
Greece, the compressed leaves smoked as you'd smoke a
salmon, and dampened, they tell us, with goats' piss to get

the nitrogen content up. He reaches for the dangling
service-bell and says with a twinkle
— Coffee? Tea?

There is a distant buzzing from downstairs. And this
being 1972, there are no servants, so no answer. But wait.
Rachel, hooking her beringed finger through the handles
of several cups, goes off dutifully to do battle with the
rancid sink.

*Thin smell of Aatjie and Vaughn busting a pipe in the court-
yard.*

Gonna Seem White

25 January 1984

Billy's on his way to Cape Town out of Maseru, but actually his mind isn't going anywhere. It's stuck right here in this fresh-from-the-oven hot 1974 custard-yellow VW Beetle, at a hundred-and-ten to a hundred-and-twenty k's per hour. He's heading in a southwesterly direction, slightly into the sun now. It pours in through the dirty windscreen and butters his hands with heat. Through the endlessly repeating Karoo. There's a dead dragonfly stuck in the mechanism of the left windscreen wiper, metallic blue, with only one wildly vibrating wing left.

Eat your heart out Lalique, this one's for real. Ah, De Doorns in just thirty k's exactly. Let's see ... at an average of a hundred-and-ten that'll be, look down at watch, say about ten to fifteen minutes. No, a little more.

He pats the dash of the car, muttering a word of praise, encouragement.

Heeoo! but this black plastic gets hot! Left buttock going numb now, shift over onto the right, but that one was used up twenty minutes ago. Straighten back, ah, pushing against the wheel. Big sweatcircle under each arm.

What's the silly thing called? Milometer way back then but kilometerometer doesn't seem quite right. Hang on, odometer! But that must be for measuring smells. 'Excuse me, sir. We've got someone from pollution monitoring on the line here, and he claims that the board meeting is reaching more than two hundred Gauss on the odometer. They're going to come in to

*investigate.' 'That's all right Smithers, just deny everything.'
... Let's see, 40204 will be the next balanced number if you
don't count the tenths. Though 40144 and 40140 have their
merits. What kind of symmetry would it be? A sort of concep-
tual one, because the little numbers don't make actual mirror
images, but the repetition is there. A palindrome. De Doorns
at 40137, according to the signs.*

De Doorns comes as a relief, a dropping away of bore-
dom: the border of two ecologies, the beginning of the
Western Cape, with the dryness left behind. It comes with
a feeling of having almost arrived.

Maseru Schmeru.

He's out of the car at the filling station, stretch, running
on the spot, over to the Wimpy for a can of Fanta (hates
Coke). Billy stands on the oilstained concrete watching the
attendant check tyres, keeping his eyes down. There's no
Maseru-style direct look or greeting that says *Khotso**, this
is white South Africa where the streets are made wide for
turning the wagons. When they'd explained that to him as
a kid he'd looked around for wagons, and, seeing none
had decided that this was another of those little lies told to
children to shut them up.

*But it must have been a lie, 'cause wagons shouldn't turn,
but keep going, the Trek never stops. And those who turn
become Pillars of Salt, Soutpilare. Soutpiele, the ones who
look back. Not one foot in England and one in South Africa
and cock hanging in the briny deep like the folk etymology
goes, rather poor old Lot's wife grieving for what have
become the radioactive wastes of Sodom. And Gomorrah.
Which must by extension have been the decadent British Cape.*

> *Keep on trekkin' mama,*
> *Trekkin' till the break of day.*
> *Keep on trekkin' mama,*
> *Trekkin' yer blues away. Hey!*

* Peace.

— It's finished the tyres my boss.

— Thank you. Oh, and ... I'm not your boss. I'd rather be your friend, if that's okay.

He looks at Billy steadily. Big smile.

— Eh. Yes my baasie. Thank you.

Stare him long in the eye, say Khotso, *say anything, don't get in the car, but there I am in the car, starting, full tank, costing roughly that dude's weekly income.... Out onto the road.*

Cape Town's gonna seem white. To me. After Lesotho, my whole life seems white. Even Maseru was white enough, but hell, any small gathering of friends in or out of anyone's home was black there, with a few of the others. Tokens. How many of Laura's friends were black? The maid?... no friend she. How many of mine? Hmm ... Aatjie and Farieda, for sure, haven't seen them for nearly ten years.... Must look them up when I get to the Cape. And there's all the Maseruites, but they don't count. Why not? 'Cause it's a special case, 'cause I'll probably never see them again. Andrew, from the Art Centre days, and Casey from the Anglo DP shop. I phoned her and said:

— Laura, honey, I'm bringing a friend from work home for supper. Casey from Ops. Great guy, he's one of the Friday bunch. Cook something good will you. Of course I'd cook but we'll only get home around six or so.

The look on her face when I come in with Casey, six foot of pitch-black Sowetan. There I am in front to intercept it, and it only lasts a fraction of a second.

— Hi, come in. You must be Casey. I've heard all about you.

— Really? I hope not. And you are surely Laura. So pleased to meet you.

He holds out his hand and gives her a one-two-three handshake, with thumb grip, like old connections. She's expecting him to be overwhelmed by the middle-class opulence, but I happen to know that the salary he draws is almost as good as mine, if not better. In the sitting-room, beers all round.

And after he'd left in his Corvette Stingray (having been whiter than the Omo washing all evening), she looked pissed off and a little drunk.

— Why didn't you tell me he was black?

— What would you have done? Made *phutu**?

— Oh, fuck off. You know what I mean. He wasn't very impressed with the spaghetti. I could tell. They probably don't eat it. I was so embarrassed. When he cut it up.

And there I sit quietly feeling my ulcer. Shit. And another wall tumbling in the already ruined structure of our affair. Four years. What would Casey make of all this? How much longer?

Four and a half months, as it turned out. It's so hard to separate, even when there's no love. Even when there's no lust.

Here's Worcester now, Karoo Gardens on the right, little town with its steeple. Engine staying cool. There are three kids playing near the road, and the game seems to involve the big ones trying to push the little one into a ditch. Gone, into the rear-view, into the past.

God, we're white. That's what Maseru's given me. My own cowardly whiteness. Thanks. There was also Jackson. Jackson Zwide. From the Art Centre days. In Maseru six months ago.

Just popping in to say hello to Harry. Down from the Hotel Albert, run by shady Mediterranean types with fingers in some weird diamond dealing, out past the whores in the whorebar, into the high dry frost-cold air. Roll collar up, wrap scarf … over the road and around the big stupid Basotho Hat. The whole hat a thatched tourist shop thrusting up two stories and housing the same junk offered to foreigners anywhere in southern Africa. Blah. Down the hedged road towards the

---

* Thick maize porridge.

*Holiday Inn, an Alsatian rushes out to the end of his leash in a
frenzy of uncontrolled barking. Nip into a side-street, through
the door in the wall, clipped lawn in here like a bowling-green,
the same fine grass. Light's on in his cottage, the top of the
stable door's open. The walls are old quarried stone, from the
days when the mason's craft, brought by missionaries, was
practised in all these hills. Open the door, barge in calling —
Harry, it's me.*

A heavily built, tall man unrolls himself from the couch,
holds out a hand the size of a welder's glove.

— Howzit. I'm Sipho.

He takes the hand. *Jesus, he doesn't let go.*

— I'm Billy. Howzit.

He's just standing there looking into Billy's eyes,
holding onto that unresisting hand. Relaxing his body into
an unarmed-combat slouch, ready for everything. He says

— What do you want?

— Uh, Harry, I'm looking for Harry.

His left hand gesturing innocence. At which point this
other guy, hovering over there with a beer in Billy's pe-
ripheral vision says

— Bill? Billy Marks?

— Yeah. Me.

— Hey, man. Don't you remember me. Jackson. No,
man, Sipho, I know him.

A cool-spade Maseru accent, very cosmopolitan.

— Mister Zwide! What the hell are you doing here?
Last time I saw you, you were lurking in the CAP dark-
room buggering up all your lovely pictures from Gugs.

Sipho lets go of the the hand, briefly squeezing Billy's
forearm in a sailor grip, smiles. And the rest of the evening is given to nostalgia. Jackson (now Themba) and Bill
discovering more and more common past, becoming better
friends than they ever had been. Exiles. Sipho sits taciturn,
on his fourth or fifth Long Tom. Billy found out later that
he was the one who'd sat with a machine-gun, one of those

big ones on a tripod, out in front of his house when the
last raid came. His wife and three kids in there under the
bed. And he'd held them off. Themba says

— I'm with the Congress now. Can't go back. Not till
we fix things up.

— Do you really want to go back? To live there? Now?

— It's my home, man. My mother's got my kids. Who
doesn't want to go home? I want to come home singing.
We're going to. Sooner than you think.

*Maseru. A world of intrigue, on the Aid hustle. Nevermind
getting the project to work. Nevermind the jobs you may be
creating or working in. The thing to do is take Mr Nyathe to
the Hilton up on the hill, sit in delicious five-star luxury by the
pool and watch that young jet-black girl's body slide into the
water. Drops pearling the finely plaited ridges of her hair. Sip
beer. Everything here is beer, the cans filling the eroded
dongas, shining imperishable alloy on every path. And slip
him a grand in a fat wadded envelope, under the table. He and
only he can swing the LNDC grant, soothing World Bank
funds into pockets. Mr Nyathe is plump and affable, with a
little moustache and square gold-rimmed specs. Comes from
Cradock in the Cape, joined the PAC in '59. Escaped '61, and
worked his way up the Civil Service ladder here, negotiating
the interplay of tribal and managerial with the amphibian ease
of a cormorant. And perhaps he is one, a cunning black-
feathered fishing-bird. When three o'clock comes and it's time
to start ending the meal, nothing has changed. An invitation to
a party, a feast. The jet girl leans on the balcony railing,
staring down on the little town through expensive shades.
Nyathe's face is made of old cast stove-iron.*

De Doorns is gone, shrinking in the rear-view. Road
and valley vanish by a trick of perspective. He crawls
through the tunnel choking in fumes from a pantechnicon,
up the last hill then swoops into the pass, engine off, running on brakes, a VW glider curving down and down into
the lush bosom of Cape Town's basin. The grapes are ripe

and being harvested by convicts with big wicker baskets. Tractors and roller-pigeons roll. Two shafts of sunlight pierce a cloud: Hollywood spotlights, triangulating on the sun.

The Morning with Bullet Hands

30 October 1972

Light comes to the house, first light moving in on the cool wind. It comes in from the east, pouring into the bowl of the city, filling it gold and pink, pouring like milk onto cornflakes. The cool of the night rolls back down towards the sea, slowly and with gusting hesitations.

Jessica lies in her bed, the blanket pushed down and crumpled. The cool of her shoulder, covered only by the sheet, makes her shrug down and hunch forward. A strand of her hair is caught between her lips.

She's not sleeping not waking not in a dream, sweating in clammy sheets. Outside a car starts, a police siren shrieks, footsteps rattle louder and fade out, a voice sings. Two people come talking, nearer now, she can't make out the words.

One leg out, no, cold. Can't make out the words. The words turn a folded cloud white rolling. Bank of clouds heap on heap, bank, I'm sorry miss ah ... Miss Winter ... Winter the account is overdrawn by an amount of white clouds, can't make out the words.

Machine-gun belt of words slamming one. By. One. One. By. One. Through thought tube firing down the tunnel, dark tunnel, here comes a word, *a word called wing, a word called wound, a word called alpha, a word called Jessica, a word called sleep. Click, ram into the firing chamber, drop the pin, squeeze the trigger the legs, a word called legs. Squirt out shove out the empty shell of the word, bouncing rolling. And the fired wing, wound alpha Jessica sleep, soars tears through cloud blue, outside the light is coming, the light! The light steals into the room on bullet hands. Don't look, the pillow, hard old dead duck pillow and his body here, here. Winter the amount, the money the money there's no money and outside the oak tree is in the morning, a bird is it a starling? On the roof a clatter on the sine-waves of tin. The morning is sitting on the end of the bed, on cloud starling legs. On bullet hands. The morning is looking down into my eyes. Don't look at where he lies clouded round and round in sleep sweet starling noise, roof, scratching pecking, woodpecking.*

The morning smiles with teeth of the sun. The clock laughs and there is waking in its rattling throat.

Jessica, it's seven-thirty in the morning of spring. Click the alarm-clock off. Look at Vaughn lying asleep, sweet boy's head, the hair long and dark, a tufty beard. There's a line of drool running from his mouth to make a dark spot on the pillow. He twitches in a dream. — Who are you? — Don't touch him now, you can look. Under the crocheted cover, under the folds of blanket and sheet he's a warm body with strong shoulders, feel his heat.

Slide out of the bed, for whole long seconds stand naked watching his sleep till the goose-bumps come from the cold. Stretch, a dancer's pose, and find the Indian cotton shawl to wrap around, tuck into the top like this, just near the armpit. Now the bathroom: lavatory first and the black plastic seat cold on your bum and thighs. There are beige and terracotta Victorian tiles smooth under feet, you can feel the sand still there from St James beach. Wash your face and soothe the wrinkles coming around your eyes. Go to the mirror, look at your dark red hair, four or five grey now, look at your shoulders, chest, ribs. Put your hands over your breasts, push the morning cool nipples down with your palms. Breathe, cough. Get the toothbrush, it's over there, and they've been using it. Never mind. Toothpaste crumpled without a cap. There's blood in the white foam spit. Spit. Rinse.

Now you go back to the bedroom, where he's rolled over into your shucked-off warmth. You're Psycho's most popular lecturer, put on your teacher's clothes: his cotton underpants, your calf-length skirt, bra, the cream silk Wild West blouse from mother, with hummingbirds embroidered below the collar and those, the flat dancing-shoes. Comb out the hair, thirty strokes on the left thirty on the right. Mirror.

Go down through the sitting-room where Billy and Cheryl lie on a single matress: she a koala-bear hugging him, a tree. Her dirty bare foot is poking out, with the toe just touching the floor. Smell what last night has become in the morning: incense, old ashtrays, damp wall must. His metal-frame kitbag has fallen over, a ball of socks rolled out. Billy's boots, the ones with beige and red Paisleys lie, tipped over on the discarded clothes. There is a pair of knickers hooked on a cowboy heel.

From what was the maid's room, you can hear Nick's hacking bronchitis cough going on and on, paused by great heaves for air.

And here's the procedure for making coffee:

a: Go to the kettle and open the lid. The kettle has no water.

b: Unplug the kettle and take it to the sink.

c: Move the stewpot and four old cups onto the table, in order to make room for the kettle under the tap.

d: Fill the kettle. The water comes out too hard and splashes you.

e: Plug it in again, switch on.

f: Find a cup. The cuphooks have no cups on them, so get one of the cups from the table.

g: Wash it with cold water until your fingers squeak against the inside.

h: Rinse it. Find a dishcloth. There's one on the back of

that chair. Dry the cup with the cleanest part.

i: By now the kettle is singing. Go through procedures f: to h: with a teaspoon.

j: Spoon one and a half teaspoons of instant coffee into the cup. The cup is a willow-pattern one.

k: Go to the fridge for milk. There is none. Look in the bottom of the cupboard where you've hidden milk-powder. Go through procedures f: to h: with a mug for mixing the milk.

l: By now the kettle's boiling.

Billy comes through in red skants, his body thin and cold. He stands near the counter so that you can't see the bulge of his waking erection.

— Morning, Jess, thought I heard someone in here.

— Morning. I'm making coffee if you want some.

— I'll come now. Shit, look at this mess. I'll do something about it today, I swear.

He sidles past you, keeping it facing away, towards the back door and the outside lavatory. There is a foamy sound of pissing and hoiking phlegm. Nick's quiet now. Billy sprints back through to shamble among the heap of clothes. Get two cups. Drink the coffee without saying anything.

— What's the time?

— About ten to eight. What are you doing up so early?

— I dunno. Like I hardly slept. Vaughn and Arn had those funny red pills and they do weird things to your sleeping patterns.

— You and your funny red pills. The red plague ...

— No, it was lekker. Really.

He's raking the mushrooms off his tongue with his teeth. Finish the coffee, two gulps. Hot.

— Promise you'll do something about this? Promise.

— Scout's honour, mom.

Leave it, ignore it. Go. Picking up your bag, the heap of papers not looked at by the foot of the stairs. The bus to

campus'll be along in twelve and a half minutes. The beha-
viourists are waiting for you up on the hill. Go.

And she walks out into the morning street. There are
commuters, one with shaver going. She remembers the
time Crazy Case Lucas stood down by Riebeeck Square, a
dingy tramp shouting:

— You're all mad. Mad! Look at you, you all hate it! I
can see you hate it. Admit it, you're mad! You don't have
to work, you're mad! — On and on.

She keeps walking, down the hill past the cars stacking
up at the Long Street Baths: metal-flake Valiants, Ford
Cortinas.. *Cars golden and phallic, phallic metallic, or
more like sperms thrusting, pushing, jostling in their stream
down to town looking for the ovum money.... Shut up.*

*Girls who get annoyed at phalluses never mention Freud.
Picture palaces, long standing, but prefer the motion of
girls....* And here's the exhaust-gas diesel bus pulling in,
full of students. Eyes in every window. Watching.

Square everything up neatly on your lap. A report on
the behaviour of hamsters allowed to breed indiscrimi-
nately in a cage measuring one meter by one meter. Statis-
tical tables at the back.

*Old research, boring. Try Reich, what rhymes with Reich?
Leich Meich Teich nothing. They'd rather get hung, than
think about Jung.... They're doing quite fine, without men-
tioning Klein.... Shut up! Vaughn's still asleep. And Arnold
and Nick asleep coughing, coughing, and everyone ... but
Billy mooching about my house bet he won't touch a dish,
coming in the study drugs drugs drugs not that the odd little
toke isn't.... Back's tight again, a pillar of steel cables, tables
please refer to the tables in appendix C, the incidence of
aggression among male hamsters is thus probably inversely
proportional to the drugs drugs bastard called me Mom me
mom me mommy mommy Shut up! Arnold, weird Arn came
and watched me sleeping just loomed over and when I opened
eyes there all tall with yellow teeth and a sort of radiant love*

schmove above watching me sleep eyes all feely about me little leeches Arnold fool I reach up and pull him down never never. Arnold Fool. Vaughn laughing eyes all wild and stary — He loves you everyone loves you, singing — All ya need is love da da da *— They get quite annoyed at the mention of me me me.* All you need is da da da love. *First tut: Brain Chemistry and Function shit. The kitchen, cook us a meal cook us, Emile, Howsabout hash brownies the hash Ned brought back from Denmark, cook us rice food We'll come help* we'll do it can I help can't I do that? *Vaughn bouncing bouncing kangaroo, all that child-raving energy, chanting —* LSD is good for ME, LSD is good for ME *— Help me in my weakness....* Shut up. *Bus along twisty-wisty De Waal Drive full of students cool hip students shy withdrawn ones straight ones in sensible clothes pimply boy with his ginger fringe in his eyes, clutching books, holding knapsacks togbags duffelbags. Big bellbottoms, long skirts circle-cut skirts, jeans jeans jeans denim jackets trimmed with that beautiful tapering waist. Quiet morning talking kids, bus-noise changing gear.*

Sea Blue Eyes

14 May 1986

He's ruling neat lines on the scheduling chart when Caroline's voice comes distorted through the intercom

— Bill, there's someone here to see you from a firm called Timeman.

— Oh, that must be the guy with the time management systems. I'll see him in the boardroom.

— He's female.

— Well, hold your thumb up in the way of the female bits and send him in. I'll be there in fifty seconds. And organise some coffee. Please.

When he gets to the boardroom, she's waiting by the door. He's already holding out his handshake.

— Hi, I'm Bill Marks....

He recognises her. There's an effort of facial control, an effort of tongue control as her cool dry hand is in his.

— Sue Green. Pleased to meet you.

Pulling out a chair — Have a seat, make yourself comfy. Caroline'll bring some coffee in a sec — he can feel the blush rising to his face, a reflex finger going to loosen the collar. *Sue Green. But your eyes are Sea Blue. Years back, how many years?* He'd never spoken to her, though he'd sat on the same bus every evening and looked at her without fantasy. Just looked. She's not his kind of beautiful but she locks perfectly into some inner pattern. Mouse hair, straight, sculpted nose and lips. *Ah yes it's in the lips.* She'd read intelligent books on the bus; the first time she'd

been reading *I, Claudius* and his secret name for her had
been Claudia. Cloudier.

— Well, let's see what, er, you're from Time Management?

— The firm's called Timeman.

— Whatever. Let's have a look. Ta. My cards're in my
desk. I'll get one later.

She slides a heavy plastic-bound folder out of her briefcase, smooths her skirt over her thighs. Thighs. She's
smiling slightly, does she remember? He'd found an offcut,
a snippet of pink ericas discarded by the flower sellers:
adrenalin throbbing, fought with himself about giving it to
her, all the way to his stop. Finally, as he was getting off,
shaking past her not wanting to look, he'd tossed it into
her lap and fled. After that she'd met his eyes unwaver-
ingly, and he'd always looked away. How many years ago?

*She must have changed but she looks the same and I must
be projecting viciously. Glenda'll have something to say about
it when I go on Monday. What's this? Concentrate, William.
Time management. You get one of these pages for every day,
as well as those. Yeah. These at the back are the monthly ones.
There are the week-planners. Look like a waste of time, more
forms to fill in don't tell her.*

— Great, great. This all looks pretty neat. Pretty neat.

The demonstration rolls on, smooth as golden syrup.
She's got her patter down fairly well, but he isn't respon-
ding, is missing the cues.

— How do you manage your time at the moment,
Mister Marks?

— Please, call me Bill. Otherwise I might think you're
referring to my granddad. I make a list. Then I start at the
top. I usually get about a third of the way down when the
bell goes.

— Bill, that's exactly what I used to do. Make a list,
when I got round to it. But the Timeman Planner allows
you to prioritise, to sort out ...

He can hear the rehearsal, the hours and hours spent in one of those windowless training rooms, with the white formica tables. There'd be overhead projectors, slides, a talk from the National Sales Manager Himself.

— Look, my brief is to just kind of see what's on the market for the whole firm. And I like what I see here, it looks sortof, well, efficient and, er ...

Glancing down at his watch, adrenal pressure speeding, palms getting sweaty, fear: this is fear.

— Christ! It's twelve fifty-two already. Um, look, erm can-I-buy-you-lunch? Or something?

Fool, blown it, blown it, sexual harassment in the office, She's probably married, no, no ring. My hands are shaking, what if she remembers me clumsy boychild on the bus, stay cool stay looking cool. Blownit Blownit Blownit Blownit Blownit Blownit ...

— Thank you. That's very kind. We can sort this out later.

The folder goes back into the briefcase. She wears pearls, a long string wound around twice, and a silver brooch in the form of a winged mermaid. Short nails, white tights. His stomach a hard monkey-ball of rope. — With you in a mo. — *Fetch jacket, make sure the cheque-book's there, trot back, usher through reception, hold the door open, after you with a slight bow, heart slowing down now.* The fear is still cold but there's hot excitement too.

Forget about the lunch. The lunch is nothing. They discovered things about each other. She's thirty-five, he one year and three months younger. Both read, both like good wine, and so on through the catalogue of all the inanities of wooing that grease the world on its pole. Billy's doing it again, thinks the signs are ... well, some of the signs are, that she is too. He keeps seeing her face differently, from other angles. Nevermind she's not Vogue cover material, has a pimple by the corner of her mouth, nevermind. Forget the lunch, at the end of which they've made an ar-

rangement for a supper, and her last words as they part
are

— Oh, by the way, in case you were wondering. I did
remember you. I was engaged in those days.

He's told her about the book, she wants to see. Yes, yes
anything, but he's worried. *It may be crap. The Peter
fellow has no real character. A cutout. The woman, well,
she's not real either. What is she?*

*A man goes from the world of the future to another
planet. He is an anthropologist and has come to study
what has been described as a particular sect in the
southern area of one of the southern continents. This other
planet is not homogeneous, and is not an allegory of the
earth. It is diverse and complicated, with all the different
societies, ecologies, economies, systems and so on which
might realistically be found in such a place. He is looking
at one tiny part of it. The capital is large and crude,
heavily technologised.*

*He meets a woman in this village who is a teacher, a
'wise old woman'....*

Blah blah. But what about Peter? Billy knows all sorts of
things about him, where he was born, raised, what his parents did, but he resists letting Billy into his private core.

*He is stiff and formal but only in manner. As an anthro-
pologist, he does really want to engage with his material,
but his own alienation prevents this, to an extent.* Billy
can't come to grips with him, he's created someone who is
closed, and can't open him without paradox. When he
does show feelings, they're so abstract!

*I'm slowly beginning to pick up a sense of their history
from conversations here and there, and finally working out
how to use the datacrystal. The community is nearly two
hundred years old! They left Tanmer in the north, as
Mylia told me, 'Four hundred people. Hardly enough to*

form two stable communities. A mixture, workers, intellec-
tuals, even some priestesses of the Matrifax.' She laughs.
'We had then the same rule that we have now: the equality
of the exchanges. Any person could challenge or test the
meaning of what was happening. The fights and argu-
ments! There were even killings.' Gradually two villages
were built, here in what was wilderness, eroded soil,
where, the few locals thought, spirits and a sort of goblin-
like creature lived. They had no leaders, because the single
rule would not allow leaders, but a system of teachers
evolved across the next hundred years. A system of knowledge keepers.

   Anyone could be a teacher, if they had things to teach,
and all had. But any teacher who attempted to oppress, to
violate with knowlege the balance of the exchanges, would
soon find that students were going elsewhere. I am putting
this all very badly. There are no teachers or students here,
but our poor burdened words are the ones that come
closest to describing the intricate and involved business of
growing up and living here. The word Guru has often oc-
curred to me, but is too suggestive of a dominating
relationship, with all the power on one side, obedience on
the other. A word first used in a country of kings.

   How shall I put it? What shall I say about her, whom I
have freely chosen as teacher? Her function here is difficult to define, because she does so many things, most of
which may be described as 'work'. But also she is a bearer
and expander of knowlege, specifically in the area of the
exchanges. A sort of social ecologist. People ask her questions, and there are three who seem most devoted, who
may become, in turn, her successors. I have watched them
in heated argument, and have never seen her become
unyielding, refuse to concede something for her dignity's
sake. Her dignity is vast and non-existent. Perhaps vast because it is not there. She is always learning, from the
others, from the shape and complexity of the community,

from the datacrystal, even from me!

I think I am falling in love with her. This bland assertion I have found hard to write down, harder to think. She is old, and, by my standards, not beautiful. But I get side-tracked. I was writing about their history.

Their history is a history of forms, of growth and of a peculiar and delicate relation to the state. By now there are thirty-two villages who follow the rule of exchanges. There are twelve in the area. There is another pocket of them several hundred kilometres to the east. And over-seas, in Nimar and Tanor-niv there are communities. But it was here that it started. Thirty-two settlements, several thousand people may sound like a lot, but on an entire planet it's very few. All are connected, all share and ex-change. All use the datacrystal, a solid-state light com-puter, which is, I think, located here. I find it hard to assimilate the fact that this planet had a form of computing when ours was first learning to cross an ocean.

When I asked him about their history, Eenirh told me the following story:

THE STORY OF THE TEACHER OF CONTEMPLATION AND THE TEACHER OF WEAPONS

There was a teacher of contemplation who moved about the country. An old and wise man, he never stayed for long in one place. On a certain day, he was sitting in the sun, watching the wind playing on the surface of a river, when he was confronted by a similar wanderer, a teacher of weapons.

'I would test the equality of our exchanges,' she said, and laid a fighting-blade in front of him.

'The wind moves over the water, making little

waves, and the water is never still. But do the waves move, or the wind? I know for a fact that the water only goes up and down, up and down and the waves are an illusion of moving,' he said, and kneeling before her he gave the blade back.

'And yet after the wind has passed over a puddle all day the water is not there, having been carried away in her womb. Come, old man. I shall fight with you.'

'That great weapon on your back, do you keep it sharp? May I see?'

She held it for him to feel. He ran his thumb down the edge, drawing a little blood. 'Do you use it to fell trees? Or for cutting wood to burn?'

'Never. This blade is nearly seven hundred years old.'

The old man sat still and stared out over the water. 'I am a tree. If you stay with me, I shall show you what I know of the way of contemplation, and you will teach me to keep an edge so sharp that it draws blood at the lightest touch. But I think that a great blade like that is useless if it cannot cut wood.'

She put her weapons back about her and squatted down to watch the wind moving over the water. After a day and a night had passed, she rose up and stretched and said, 'Come, we shall find you a fine whetstone down by the river and grind it smooth.'

The old man rose, and from that time they were like the wind and the water and none could tell whether the water moved, or the wind.

The story worried me, and still does. I could get none but the most cryptic comments from him. Had it really happened? 'Yes, of course. It happens all the time.' What

*had it to do with history? With their history? 'Ah, if you're
looking for facts you must go to the crystal.'*

*'Are there really teachers of weapons? Your people
seem peaceful to me.'*

*'We defend the matrices. We shield life, which is itself a
shield.'*

*Urnn, I quite like the sort of myth story. Wonder if it really
is wise, it feels more like a dream. She'll go for it. I can see her
reading it. That name Eenirh, though. Somehow the irritating
little alien terms don't come out right. Keep a list of names, a
list of possible words. Tanith, Vasir, whatever. Only use the
good ones, the ones that seem right. Oh, shit, would Tshaba-
lala seem right?*

Kanonprop

19 May 1986

She should have a beard and one of those reclining couches. A chaise-longue. That always sounds like a cough lozenge.... Glenda, I really go for your horn-rimmed spectacles. Glenda, I think your 'Tell me about your childhood' stuff is corny as hell.... Tell me about your childhood, and it had better be good.... I'm thinking in clichés again. Where were we?

— Let's see, now. His name was *Kanonprop*[1], yes definitely. I can't remember the real name at all.... Just *Kanonprop*.

— Never mind his name. Try for the face.

— Aah ... I think it was Blignaut, there were quite a few of them about and they all looked a bit alike. I think they came down from Graskop. He was in Grade One, that's your Sub A. I was in Grade Two. I should have been bigger than him, but I wasn't, I was smaller, thinner.

— D'you remember where he got that name? *Kanonprop*?

— Well, my friend Nigel said it was because of his funny round head and supershort hair, which made him look sort of like a cannonball. His family had *kroes*[2] hair, I think. But I had the impression that it was because he appeared at school with a massive *goen* during the marble season. His father was a shunter or some sort of railway worker and he got this bloody huge ballbearing. Like that. I don't really re-

1 Cannon wadding; by extension a cannonball.
2 Frizzy.

member it, apart from a general impression, you know.

— Let's come back to the fights.

— I know where they happened. Under a tree. I think it was a syringa, though I can remember the mango more clearly. Mr Koorzen, he was the vice-principal, always parked his Kombi under the mango tree, it was a big one with shiny dark-green leaves. Every year the tree would try to bear fruit. Mangoes don't really have flowers, to speak of. Just little lumpy sort of greenish-white things. But the tree would get fruit every year, and every year the kids would be up the tree to tear them off before they could even begin to have the faintest tinge of ripeness. You know, green, totally green. They taste like acid and turpentine, not something people ought to eat. Those mangoes weren't even allowed to reach half their natural size, they didn't even develop proper strings to stick in your teeth. I ate them too. One year some of the boys put sand in Mr Koorzen's petrol tank.

— The fights, Bill.

— Oh, yeah…. It's funny, I can't even remember what we fought about. Not one thing. Nothing. But every day we'd meet under that tree. After school and before the bus. I had a small brown suitcase; textured, with rusty round rivets holding it together. It smelled of rancid butter and ink and stuff. Er … yes, and then the fight would break out. Always the same. Kanonprop would just, sort of, well … fuck me up. It was terrible.

— Yes, go on.

— Well, I don't know. I mean, ja, it must have been really terrible.

— And what did it *feel* like? That's what we're really interested in, isn't it?.

— I, er.

— Try this, here, come and sit over here in the other chair. Yes, that's it. Now close your eyes and breathe. Nothing else, just breathe. We'll come back to all this stuff

in a moment. In. Out. Deeply. Deeper. Feel how it goes all
ragged when you take it really deep?

— Mmm ... okay.

— Just stay with that for a while.

*Ja, she's right, it sort of vibrates down at the bottom there
when I take it really deep. In, tikka tikka tikka. Out. The
fights. It is weird. That I can't even remember his face properly. Haven't thought about it for years. Or ever really.*

— Deeper, you're going shallow.

— Ng.... *In, tummy going forward back forward back
feel it stretch shrink out in ...*

— Now imagine you're Kanonprop. Sitting there with
your eyes closed. Feel into it for a while. We've got time.

— Hang on, I can't even remember the guy's face.
There's nothing at all about him. I told you. Nothing. You
can't just expect me to ...

— That's okay. I only want you to play with the idea for
a while, you can start by imagining such a character. What
might it be like to be him? That ought to be easy enough,
you needn't go far, just make a start.

— That really sounds quite patronising. Making it easy
for the moron or something.

A long silence.

— I'd have to imagine an eight or nine-year-old's space.
That's not so easy.

*That playground. Brown, with bits of kikuyu grass and a
few long wispy veld grasses good for pulling out the seeding
part and sucking the soft green stem. The tree ... that was near
the shooting-range in the playground. Cars, Dinky Toys and a
few Corgis and those heavy solid little Fangio racing-cars with
so-smooth oiled rubber wheels ... 3-in-1 oil on rubber, a
special secret smell gathering green blazer-lint in the pocket.
The cars are for racing down the corrugated iron of the firing-
range shelter, a sort of low roof over a row of low narrow
brick walls where the big boys must once have lain to shoot
their .22 rifles at the targets down on the clay bank over there.*

*Big boys with hairy legs and short khaki school trousers, lying
in those cool dark red-brick tunnels with the smell of earth and
cordite or whatever and squinting down solid heavy guns.
Crack. Hardly any recoil. Crack. The bullets have nearly all
been excavated by now, the doppies incorporated in games by
smaller boys (never girls), whistled shrilly into, dropped,
trodden and worked into other backyard and farmyard earth
in a sort of brass diaspora to all the surrounding area, for
miles. Actually not only brass. There were two kinds, brass
and silvery, probably nickel. The nickel ones rarer but not
more desirable, just different. Lined up on the white window-
sill at home, backed by bougainvillaea: Ten, fifteen brass
ones, three or four nickel ones, a big .303 shell and a shotgun
cartridge that still smelt of being shot, of Dad potting at guinea
fowl, holding the smooth cool butt against his cheek ...*

— Have you got it?

— No, I'm having a bit of trouble feeling into it.

— What were you thinking?

— About the schoolyard. There was a shooting-range
there.

— This other boy, d'you think he played there?

— Sure.

— Well, try to feel him playing there. You should be
able to place him now.

*Yes, I could get into the feeling of having those big ears.
Bakore. I'm hanging about that shooting-range, and it's
hot. Feel the two-o'clock subtropical sunlight shining on
those ears, radar dishes catching solar flares, cosmic rays....*

— Getting it?

— It's hot. He's got big ears.

— D'you think you can say that in the first person?

— Sure. Er, I've got big ears. That sounds like a sort of
discrimination. Earism or something.

— Don't judge it. What it feels like is the important
thing. This kid, with his big ears. You.

— I already said hot. The sun is shining on the ears, on

my neck. It's about two in the afternoon, summer. I've got
a short-sleeved khaki shirt and khaki shorts on. Teesav.
Sanforised and shrunk. Bare feet, I've kicked my sandals
off. I can feel my feet going plap plap on the packed reddish earth. But now I'm playing a game. I can't step on
the ground, only on other things. A stone, another stone,
a twig, some leaves from the big tree. Up onto the roof of
the shooting-range, it's only about so high. The corrugated
iron is dark and polished smooth from years of playing.
It's a bit like the milk cans they used for bringing heated
milk at tea break. Galvanised. It feels warm from the sun.
I'm going all the way around the school and back to here
before the bus comes, without stepping on the ground. I'm
standing here and I map my journey, at least the part that
I can see. First, there's a difficult jump from here onto the
tree root. I make it to the root, which is also smoothed,
but a different kind of smooth. You understand, this all
has to be in Afrikaans, but I can't really do Afrikaans
properly, so even though I'm picturing it quite clearly, I've
been imagining the words in English.

— That's fine, fine. Carry on.

— Where was I?

— On the root.

— Oh, ja. On the root. I'm heading up to the tree then
I'll edge around it and take a longish root over to the sort
of lawn patch. But there's this little English *ou* sitting
under the tree and I think I'll *donder* him instead.

Another long silence.

— And, you know, it's funny, but I can't think of a
single reason for doing it, not one. I thought about it. It's
not because I'm Jewish, we never really stressed the fact.
I'm sure they didn't know... but I'm this little guy and I'm
going to beat this other little guy up for no reason at all.
Only because that's how it is.

— What does he seem like to you? What's he doing?

— Oh, he's just sitting there on his suitcase. He's got a

stick, and he scratches in the sand with the stick.

— Show me how he sits.

— Like this. Ja, thanks. He's doodling like this.

— He's you.

— What?

— You're him. Tell me about it.

— Oh, okay. I'm just sitting here. I don't think I'm doing anything, thinking anything in particular. I aim down the stick, no, it's not a gun, it's just a sort of looking, I used to do it all the time. Pointing and aiming squintingly down my finger, I used to feel embarrassed about it. Perspective bothered me. I couldn't work out why things got smaller.

— Try to stay in the present tense.

— Look, I really don't think we're going anywhere. I keep feeling as though I'm getting caught in a kind of slough of trivia. It's one thing to keep recalling all these fine details, or fantasising them, but I don't feel as if we're coming to grips with anything. None of it seems to make any difference. Yes, I ... I do realise that I'm being evasive.... But I'm not sure why, or what exactly I might be evading. It's weird.

... *Liar, you liar,*
your pants are on fire!
Your nose is as long
as a telegraph wire!

... *But I've sworn, sworn with a steaming breath oath to tell no-one, not you, not Sue, hardly even me. How to tell about the phone call, from a callbox, peep peep cligrink:*

— *Hello, Billy, man. It's Aatjie. Call me back have you got a pen there? Okay the number's 47-3295. Phone me now, hey. I'll wait.*

Aatjie after whatsit been four months? Pick up the phone, ringing tone, dial ... two rings ...

— *Aatjie! You bugger where are you?*

— *No, man, listen. I want you to do me a favour. I can't*

talk now. Will you meet me, it's urgent, man?

— Sure, uh well, where?

— Say, bus stop seventy-five. On the Main Road in Salt River. At nine thirty sharp. If I'm not there jus' wait, I'll come. Please Billy man. It's fucken important, you'll understand.

— Well, sure, but ...

— No, listen. Later. I'll tell you later.

— Well, ja. Nine thirty then.

— Right. See you. Thanks, hey. Cheers.

The Main Road at night, carlights smudging in the rain. Big streetscrubbing machine doing its round, scrubbing what the weather's already washed. Rain. Rain coming down puddling all the red-and-blue neon, starring the traffic lights out in reflected pools. Stuttering on the bus shelter. Water roiling the drains full, carrying chip packet, cigarette butts, winding round the tyres where the parked car steams from the bonnet. Visible breath rising and merging. An empty bus passes, the driver leaning forward as his windscreen wipers pump. Red lights get smaller. The shelter smells of piss, has POES IS KONING, JFK'S along with the usual sperming cock and spraypainted, You ANC Nothing Yet.

Nine thirty-seven. Shoes are getting wet. Shrug down into the anorak. There he comes, running. He's wearing a grey tracksuit, hood up. Running shoes. He's really soaking. Down Queen's Park Road, turn at the factory, Rex Trueform in red, lighting a halo on the wet hood. Over the road without looking. He's carrying something, clutched with both hands to his chest. Sees me and stops on the island, connects my eyes, then gives a fugitive look left and right, sprints for the shelter.

He stands next to me panting and starting to shiver, grips my shoulder hard. The words steam out.

— Howsit Billy.

— *All right, but fuck man, you gonna die if you stand about like that.*

— *No. I'm fine. Just fine. Don't worry. About me.*

I light two smokes and pass him one. What he's clutching to his breast is a briefcase. Black rectangular, the type that is sold as 'Executive', with combination locks. Runnetes of water slide down its plastic sides. His cold hand fumbles the cigarette to his mouth, a deep drag.

— *Listen, Billy. You were my brother. You tell this to no-one, not even your dog. Nobody. Can you do that?*

— *Ja, sure. What?*

— *Swear to God?*

— *I swear. Whatever it is, I'll shut up. Completely.*

He pushes the briefcase towards me.

— *Look after this for me. I'll fetch it soon. I'll come myself, and please make fucken sure you don't give it to anyone else.*

I take it by the handle. He puts his arm around my neck and pulls my head onto his shoulder. For perhaps two seconds we stand in this embrace. I can feel his wet hand on the big strong tendons of my neck, the terror shooting a roman candle inside me. Then he's gone, into the rain, into dark Salt River streets. I see his arms swinging as he rounds the corner at the end of the block. His footfalls are lost as the rain plays a snare on the sheet-iron roof.

In the cupboard, under the pile of blankets. Real. Waiting for me when I get home. In the cupboard under the red-and-black Lesotho blanket with the Battle-of-Britain Spitfire design. In my mind in the cupboard under the patchwork from Mom and the Lesotho blanket waiting for me to return in my mind. How can I tell her. Look Glenda, the real problem's not with school, not with my ulcer or Dad dying or any of this shit. It's actually a problem of silence or betrayal. A brother's oath. Swear.

... Liar, you liar,
your pants are on ...

— Well we've nearly run out of time. If you think you're being evasive, let's try doing it this way: you make a list during the week of things you might be evading. Anything, it doesn't matter. You know, washing the dishes, things at work, whatever. And also things in your past you don't want to look at. It can be hypothetical, we'll sift through it later. Keep it with you, at the back of your diary.

— I'll try, but I don't see the point.

She smiles broadly, her first smile this session.

— Well, put the list itself at the top. That should be a start.

— Mm, okay. See you next week, then. Are you still reading the Ken Wilbur?

— I'm nearly through, have it here next time.

The Exchanges

30 May 1986

A swirling. A rush of motion. Everything's changed. The
danger area now moves into the massive sepulchral station,
he has to dodge, run, wait, to make his way over to where
there's someone in uniform.

— Where can I get a ticket?

And there's some confusion about this, too. There are
two men now and he can't find the money: jacket pockets,
inside, only crumply old papers, waistcoat pockets, trousers. They're getting impatient and the vibes are worsening.
Shirt pocket, jacket pockets again. There's a crush of some
old dried plant, grey and tangled with pocket-lint like sage
here, soft old laundered papers. No money and the guard's
holding out a ticket: fifteen rands.

*How the hell am I going to get fifteen rands, back pockets,
jacket again, they're getting impatient, they're going to get
heavy soon. The train's already here, in the danger zone.*

— Fifteen rands? I'm only going three stations.

He produces a little heap of coins for which he's given a
yellow cardboard ticket with a bite taken out of the one
edge. The train's pulling out, there's no platform: run, run
next to a door, missed, the next door. The train's full, full
of people. A kindly looking old lady closing the door takes
the briefcase, he holds the brass rail, one hand, feet off
the coaly ground now. Hoist, up, in, the door slams.

*Right, now where's the briefcase? Jam of people, no, no
haven't seen it, bodies pressing. Shit, gotta get it. Push past*

*them, seals wriggling on an ocean rock, down into the aisle.
Two, three, four seats up, people everywhere, standing, sitting. The light's late dusk and getting darker, colours all burnt
sienna and amber. I'm getting angry now, pushing people out
of my way. There they are: two women sitting at a table. They
had it! Them. Sit down next to them.*

— Where is it? My briefcase? Where?

There's no answer but a sphinx smile. The further one,
brunette, says

— It was sub-standard.

He takes the first woman by the head, pushing her face
down onto the table, holds it there and lightly hits her
nose down against the top.

— Where?

Bash, harder. — Where is it? — Bash harder.

— We don't know. It was sub-standard.

— What do you *mean* sub-standard? It's my whole life.
My whole life's in there.

The guard's arrived. — Tickets! — He can feel it in his
trouser pocket, in there with all the crumply papers, old
till-slips, crushed cigarette packet. Sub-standard.

— It's in my briefcase. Ask them, they've got it.

Holding her by the neck, he hits her face on the table
again, bam.

— Where?

He reaches over to the other, grabs her by the hair,
pulling head back and exposing her white neck. *Pull till
she chokes, makes a little sound like an animal needing air.*

— Where is it? Thieves. My life, my ticket.

Now he feels the briefcase shoved under from another
seat, touching his knees, safe. It's old and broken, the
leather unstitched along the top, showing parchment
colour.

The scene shifts. He's with the women on the platform,
puts his arm around the one whose nose he'd crushed into
the table. They're all friends now, all can understand, they

were joking, playing a *trick* and he was serious as hell, his life stolen away. It seems they're schoolgirls', studying for an exam. Here on the platform people herd, vendors shout food, newspaper, porters with enormous bundles skivvy past.

Mike and Lindsay are there. Mike starts saying

— They say we're back to the old-style Special Branch. Like in the early sixties. Though that's not my speciality, I'm really only interested in the period from 1912 to 1948.

And Lindsay says

— Yes, they've all got stupid again. They don't have to care how stupid they get. Everyone can be stupid now....

Billy has dozed in front of the telly, a pile of manuscript on his lap. What looks like a Dutch Reformed minister wearing a white tie on screen, sound off. Background of a lake with pines. He smiles with media compassion. Cut to a choir of girls in powder-blue robes. Blonde faces lifted to God up there, fade to a single candle. The text, in golden Gothic, rolls up the screen from the bottom.

Smashing her face into the table, holding her by the neck.... He can still feel the hair and the two big tendons and the base of her skull. He looks at his hand, nudging the heap of pages. The papers slide over each other and fall curling to the floor.

But I walked with my arm around her and she smiled at me. Who are the people in dreams? Glenda says it's all me.... And if I dream of those men beating and beating a little girl? Am I the girl? The men?

Could I just kill Mylia? Bam?

The new wall is going well. The style of building here is interesting, both utilitarian and decorative, as well as being designed, it seems, with the environment in mind. Colours are appropriate and the forms seem to suit the outcrops of rock in the area. Mylia and Darut have been laying the stones with precision, encouraging me to join in. Others move in and help for an hour or so, manual labour, but Darut is always here. He has planned the wall and so is doing most of the work, designer as well as builder. I don't think they would really understand our idea of an architect, the separation of roles.

A group of three help to hoist a stone lintel into place, Mylia guiding and pushing from below. I also pull on the block and tackle. The rope breaks and the slab of stone weighing about three hundred kilograms falls,

Can't do it. Imagine: her death living inside of me, perpetually falling under the ... there's enough dead people in there, ghosts, oh Jess.

The screen has the Flag on it, Orange White and Blue stiffly fluttering as a background to the words of *Die Stem* which slide over the screen in sedate silence.

But in the dream I walked with my arm around the girl I'd just tortured and we talked about her exams. After I'd held her head and hit her face on the table asking for my life in a battered briefcase. Is that my life? What would I find in it? Or what would I find in the cupboard, under the blankets, behind two combination locks? Two locks, they must have the same code, three four five two.... My life? Sub-standard. Everyone can be stupid now. Me. I can be stupid, like the old-style Branch. Rush out into the street and be stupid. Evil is stupid, that's why Ahriman eternally loses the battle with Ormuzd. Like hell.

He feels the stomach pain again, reaching through into his back below the shoulderblades. Gets up, stretches, lies on the floor, knees up — Naah, fuckit ... off to the kitchen for:

BILLY'S ULCER BLITZ

1: Take one Valium. For the tension, for the cause.
2: For the pain take 2 Paracetamol tablets. Be sure they're not aspirin, because that rips into the tender stomach lining like a chain-saw.

3: Take one to one-and-a-half teaspoons of any antacid with a surface anaesthetic. The gel will line the stomach and protect the internal environment. Wait fifteen minutes for this to take some effect.

4: For the acid itself:

    4.1: 1 teaspoon of bicarb in warm water, gotta watch that one, fizzing away in there like a glass of champagne. It can cause acid flashback, which is not what you may think, but the tummy's tendency to produce *more* acid if the inner environment becomes too alkaline.

    4.2: Burp. Don't lie down, squat on your haunches, great depressurising belches.

    4.3: Take 1 Tagamet. Cunning little bugger turns off the central nervous system switch that says to make the hydrochloric at all.

5: Have a hot bath. Do everything you can consciously to relax that deep long muscle that runs down from the diaphragm to the pelvis.

6: Drink some yoghurt.

7: If religiously inclined, pray. Confess your sins.

He's got as far as the deep bath, more hot, twiddling the tap with left toes till it scalds, swirling down his side. Aah. Sucking a blue clutch-pencil, papers heaped on the rim, going limp from steam. Pain teasing out into the water.

Having worked with them in the sun all day, I was stiff and sunburnt with blistered hands. The wall had progressed slowly, and Darut was fussing. I lay on my back outside and watched the unknown stars, my thoughts coming back and back to the idea of work in the abstract. Perhaps I was trying to escape the physicality of our labour, the muscle-shaking effort of lifting stone, carrying mortar. I had kept telling myself that the work was boring, coarsening, but the joking calm and obvious enjoyment of the others contradicted me.

They had sung while working, and I have translated the

song rather freely as follows:

> *How much love will satisfy a child?*
> *Pull, dogs, carry the stone.*
> *How much love will satisfy a man?*
> *Pull, dogs, carry the stone.*
> *How much love will satisfy a woman?*
> *Pull, dogs, carry the stone.*

on and on in a round, with peculiar harmonies and a rhythm which seemed to skip a beat at intervals which I couldn't predict. I think there's a game in changing it, and in picking up the new beat without stopping singing.

We ate together again. There must have been about thirty in the long eating-hall, sitting crosslegged, squatting, touching each other, talking and laughing. Mylia sat opposite me. She talked at length with Yari, about compost, the kitchen, the positioning of herbs to get the best light. The food was starchy and lightly spiced: delicious. She asked me how the wall was going, whether there'd been any problems. I told her, and also what I'd been thinking about: that I'd found the labour hard and boring.

'When I was much younger, the teacher of the exchanges was Sellae, a fine old man. He always encouraged me to think about what work is, and to feel with him the quality of mind and hands changing things. I also feel that ideas about work are useful. Certainly, thinking about these things has helped me to enjoy and maybe understand being alive.'

I fumbled to get my voice-recorder out. She gave a hand-gesture of consent. What follows is my translation, inadequate as usual. In the dining-hall, surrounded by the sounds of their meal, what she said sounded ordinary and informal. I didn't interrupt. But I am unable to recapture her simple tone while retaining the precision of her words. Where the word has been impossible, I have indicated this by means of brackets, giving my best equivalents. The word matrix, for example, can also mean both substrate and mother, depending on stress and context.

*'... [we] hold that the only source of energy for an orga-
nism is exactly in relating to its substrate (matrix, mother).*

*For us this may have some unexpected, some important
implications.*

*'What is the mother of our society, of human society?
Well, of course, the material (solid, actual) world, the
community of life. And how we see this is absolutely
straightforward: look at a human doing work, at yourself
building a wall, irrigating the field. Or look at a plant
changing light and water into the breasts of the matrix.
That is (mana?), the true exchange.*

*'Eating and breathing is work. Making love is work.
Thinking is also work, but only if it enters into the exchanges again. Otherwise it is nothing.'* She pointed across
the room at a young man who, having finished his food,
was engaged in what looked like a staring match with a
woman who could have been his sister.

*'Eenirh over there knows more about this than I do, he
teaches contemplation. Ask him some day. He'll be glad to
share time with a man who's made the journey through the
spheres. But the simple fact is that all energy comes from
the (material substrate, mother) through the (exchanges,
webs) and goes back to the mother. And the exchanges
are labour.*

*'Another way to say that is: If you don't eat and breathe
you die. Pfft. And also if you don't shit and breathe out
...'* She shrugged. *'And, if the (living animal, body) that is
society can't maintain its complexity by (interweaving) with
the mother, it must also die. Slowly, of course, because it's
big and complicated, but with the certainty of a stone
thrown over a cliff. You see we',* pointing at me, herself,
gesturing around the room, *'(individulal, unique) humans
are the (intermatrix) between our culture, our human
society, and the source of its energy. Our work is the
society's eating and shitting. All of this world turning, and*

yours too, is an unimaginably complex and finely woven web of intermatrices, of work and exchange, that pass the seed from the sun to the spirit.

'Are you following me? You must stop me if I get carried away or it seems too complicated, or if I start rambling, talking crap. And I really want to hear what you and your people have thought about this.'

'I'm getting it all in the recorder. I'll play it back and translate it later and bring you my questions.'

'It's a slow way to hold a conversation.' She seemed

The top sheet of paper slides into the water. Billy lunges to grab it and the rest go after it. Four soggy floating pages. He lies back, picks them up one at a time and drapes them over the edge of the bath, where they stick, pulls the plug out with a prehensile toe.

Later in bed he lies for an hour or so in the dark, trying for sleep like a fly bashing against a window in its effort to get at the light. Bzzz, zzz, ZZZ ... while the poor old halfwit subconscious spews up its mangled version of the last week's thoughts and terrors.

Druggists' Sundries

17 November 1972

— Come on, Jess. Come.

— No, you go on. I've got work to do.

— More marking. Naah, staircase them. The ones that land on the top stairs get the top marks. It gives a better distribution curve, if you get the throw right.

— That may be so, but you lot just fuck right off and leave me to do my work.

They go out into the dark, past the weedy little ten square feet called garden, with a wooden cable-drum and a greying broken rattan chair. The row of plaster-of-paris cast hands, all thirteen of them: Vaughn's hands making a last supper. Wrought-iron gate green and peeling, creeee, creee-dak. Out into the street-lit dark. Vaughn and Billy and Aatjie the conquering kings: kinkering Kongs.

Walking. Three people walking is a six-part heel-toe rhythm and if you listen and fit in, it becomes a Moondog cantata. Subtle.

And a pair of narrow winkle-picking boots, with acrylic stars, all colours.

> Vaughn has got such pointy-pointy boots,
> Vaughn has got such pointy-pointy boots,
> Star-stalking boots for rolling toots.
> Car goes past. The driver hoots.

And here we go, Drugs on parade, ladies and gentlemen. The three men walking down the road towards the centre of

Town are high *and getting higher and gyring and perning out out* OUT of control. *Arms linking arms to make a scrum front-line and leaning leeeeaaaannnninginging back as far as balance will take it, feels a lot further.*

Ladies, kind ladies and gents, these boys are only walking in step because their souls are similarly twisted, look at them, their will sapped, pulpy mashed minds, their courage and manhood scattered like chaff. Here is evidence of corruption, sweet sirs: men, grown men hugging each other in broad (or is it narrow?) streetlight, see, the leering look, a black man holds a white.

Hide your daughters, friends, tuck away your sons in their neat white beds. Blonde heads on pillows lie sweet with dreaming. Look look, here come the Communists, the An-archists, Bolsheviks, Nihilists ravening Socialists, drugspawn, devilspaw, catspaw, hell's maw, a bomb in every pocket. That one, the big one with the beard, he might be, madam, raging Bakunin come to life, lllleeeannnnninnnngggg back into the others' arms. Think of him, ladies, in your daughters' arms, his hands go you-know-where, go everywhere, his eyes stare out his crazy eyes, close your eyes in holy dread and weave a circle round him thrice, ladies and gentlemen.

Look at the hair, Sweet Jesus, that long hair smoothing on a man, *no man, but hide your sons away and pass your hands before their eyes, no, no! Don't let them peep!*

The druggists are coming to town today
Hurrah, hurrah,
The druggists are coming to town today
Hurrah, hurrah,
The men will cheer and the boys will shout
and the ladies they will all turn out
and we'll ALL FEEL FINE WHEN...
haaaaaa hahahaha Haaaaaa HAHAHAHA!!

The bass comes in, slow and snaky. Streak's up there onstage, big glittering red Fender Stratocaster, snow-white Davy Crockett jacket with long tassles. Now the brushed drum, slow unrelenting tropical rain. Bass weaving. Enter big deep footpedal drum thudding out a staggered beat, and now *NOW NOW* the high scream of the first blues chord, buzzing its long sustain into the room. Drumsticks now, starting paused and tentative, building building to a gunrattle on the snares. Now the lead: one huge vibrato note yelling whooping screaming. The riffs rage, faster and faster, following the drum, higher, up and up the guitar neck, dipping and twisting. Unbearable. Impossible volumes mind-stealing. Streak stock-still, only the long fingers working, and in midnote, sudden, silence. The bass again, slow and low as he moves to the mike:

> The sun will set down on the sea of deception,
> The moon will rise up on the body of lies,
> And I will look down and see my reflection:
> A young man's mind in the mirror of skies.

The band rolls in, a wave breaking on the shores of the room.

> And I want you,
> And I want you ooo ooo,
> And I want you little girl
> To be around yeah aroun'
> When they lay my ...
> Body down.

Lead break. Now he's dancing, moving, leaping over cables, swinging the Strat like a pick, over head, down to groin. Drums, drums. Curly Nina thundering, epileptic jackhammer strokes.

> There'll be dancers and jugglers and blind street
>   musicians
> There'll be tumblers and midgets, and minstrels and
>   clowns
> Yes 'n feasting and singing and drinking and laughing
> And love in the loins till the juices run down.
> And I want Yooooooo ooo ooo
> I want you little child

And you and all of you oo ooo
To come, a, round
When they lay my body down.

The whole band moving to the gleaming stork micro-
phones for the chorus, audience joining in unheard on the
oo's, and Billy can, you know, *see* the music. His eyes
closed, the patterns form and merge into bright mandalas,
into circles and tunnels. A row of BATMEN, seen from
above, a cartoon cabaret of Mickeymice ducks ducks
ducks. Arrows of light pointing in *four*, yes, that's right
four, dimensions. His hands cupped over his ears making
waaw waaw sounds open close the Music, down into it,
down past the circles of neon Mister Plod the Policeman,
past field of coals and out, out into stars, stars!

And the wind, the great wind will conquer the cities
And the waves will come in and wash over the towns.
And the stars will come down and rebuild the Garden,
Wearing the rainbow, the rainbow of sound.
And I want you oh oh oh yooooo oo
Yeah child child sweet child you,
Yes you all of you ooo oo
I want ya to come around around yes around
The day they lay my ...
Body down.

Silence poises, and the people start screaming, whistling,
cheering. *Light another cigarette.*

— Thankyou ladies and gentlemen, there will be a half-
hour break before the band comes on again — And the
record starts right away: *Led Zep, yep squeezing their
lemon.*

Streak comes over to their table up above the dance-
floor. They say nothing, just the handgrip, smile, look
stoned, drugged high tripping. The oilfilm slides light ac-
cross the dancers, *green tweaking and running into amoeba
pseudopod, yeah, it's gonna divide, there's two. Yellow
lavalamp viscera wobble over and the whole lot they.*

Tumbleswirl. They're wrong youknow, they never really guessed. The lightshow's not any sort of attempt to simulate a trip. Acid-free acid. Crap. Lightshows're a special entertainment invented by Heads, get it, and what they're meant for is entertaining other heads who just happen to be STONED. *A rarefied art form which requires a special state of mind to be properly appreciated.*

The slides overlay the oilfilm, with a real Keystone Cops movie off to the left; now in reverse. Under it all, people in kaftans, people in jeans, waistcoats, beads, minis, midis, Robin Hood costume, jerk and writhe inside the music, the big bass speakers vibrating the guts, vibrating the pelvic floor, the dance floor, the glass on the table.

To the men's room. Ammonia smell, two guys in a corner huddle conspiracy, someone else coming in, bringing sound with the open door, shutting it out. Voices raised:

— No man Nigel, give it here man.

Shit there's going to be a fight. Sidle for the door, zipping, around them, there's shouting now, the big one, Nigel, grabs the other one by the shirt. Good, the door, feel the handle, out Slam! Slam-slam, spring door. Down the concrete stairs with the little ridges on each step, mind the puke, bottom door nudge it open past the bodies, back into the warm, the big wombing rumbling sound of it all.

Who Remembers Makhno?

4 June 1986

Burning burning burning. Little houses, houses wall-
papered with labels from pilchard tins in step repeat.
Wooden houses, tin houses plastic houses, burning. Dense
smoke in the air, teargas in the air, gunsmoke in the air.
Burning burning burning. Thirty thousand people, the
human brain counts up to five before it goes to rote repetition. One two three four five many. Many people. Burning. Many little houses, with ten twelve people in them,
broken branch alleys with water and sand, with rubbish,
dead dogs bloated a feast for flies, maggots, burning. No
trees here any more, the trees all torn down for firewood
long ago, only people, houses, little and leaking; a cold
sickly wind coming through the cracks, houses, rubbish,
tired dogs heads resting on paws: burning. Great leaves of
fire, jungles of fire, labyrinths of fire wreathing round and
round. Mattress, old vermin mattress. Armchair with
tapered legs, all the hire-purchase, rand a week, two rand
a week, twenty, fifty, burning.

You take what you can get and move, what one small
person can carry. You take the hi-fi set, or the tincan
stuffed with three years' savings, the baby, you take the
baby your cousin's father's sister's child, take the ... run
run the teargas, clearing the way for them, burning. Run
down the pathway between houses, narrow narrow. One
match one torch, one milkbottle of petrol poured and the
whole lot burn, fall like cardhouses each firing the next,

great leaves of fire, jungles of fire, labyrinths of fire
wreathing round and round. Run, past the dead dog
bloated, through the mud and water in the road, past
Snowy's rusted car where two people sleep, run.

There's old Mrs Dlamini with a bullet in her, bleeding
dead she looks dead. Matthew Mpondo holding her body
the blood running out into the sand, and he's keening
high-pitched like a wild dog in the night.

Run, the teargas, eyes nose, cough fall. Get up it's okay
to cry but try not to breathe. Heat, smoke. Run. Two
years building and adding to the house, stuffing a rag in a
crack, stealing a board. The windows from the wrecking-
yard carried on Mangena's donkey car, cracking and
curling from the heat. The one asbestos sheet that was the
back wall by the big bed, bursting like gunfire as the fire
winds round and round. Run. Burning.

Comrades. The comrades have a few guns, too few.
They have sticks and fists and voices and they run and
hide and wait and move. The comrades have bright eyes,
have a wet cloth for the gas. No uniforms, each his own
uniform. Defend, hold, try to defend. Group. Talk, stac-
cato. Disperse. Run. The comrades fight back, but the
Casspirs move, booming their covering fire. And the Vig-
ilantes, the Witdoeke, move, a phalanx, a hard angry wall
under covering fire. Guns, the noise of guns.

Out into the night ... smoke and the noise of guns.

First they came for the women ... a year ago, more. Broke
up the women's organisation meetings. A few just vanished,
more were beaten up, raped.... A woman must look down
when a man enters the room, must never speak of men's
things. Work and cook, look down.

Then for the children, squadrons of them moving through.
A fist, a shoe in the face. Hold him down and smash smash
smash smash until a bit of bone shows white through the
blood. The children must not organise. No COSAS, no UDF,
no AZASO, no students' organisation. No disrespect. The bit

of bone shows white through the blood.

And now, under protection, under the shadow of the Buf-
fels, of the Casspirs, under the long dark shadow of the State,
they come. For everyone. Burning burning burning. Thirty
thousand people, averaging ten in a shack. With the white rag
on the arm, a thick stick with a railroad bolt screwed on the
end. With petrol, rag, match.

> *Have you seen that vigilante man?*
> *Have you seen that vigilante man?*
> *Have you seen that vigilante man?*
> *I been hearing his name all over the land ...*

There's nothing to do when there's nothing. Stand by
the side of the road and wait. Wait to make a connection.
Wait for a cousin, an uncle, aunt. Wait for the Casspir to
rattle past. Wait in the wind, wait in foodlines, lines for
cast-off clothes from Rondebosch and Newlands.

Brave reporters go in. If they can get permission, can
slip past the police, if they don't get shot, shot by comrades freaking out seeing a *white man*, by police, Witdoeke, security, army, jumpy kids eighteen nineteen, at
school last year. Jumpy kids reared on *die Kaffer op sy*
plek,* reds under the beds, under the floors, reds commies
total onslaught AntiChrist. Anyone moving might get shot
in the back from the top of a great high armoured car.
Shot. Gassed, eyes nose mouth asshole lungs burning
burning, run run run. Coming out with terse stories, from
the front of the Third-world War.

But what if you're not brave, just poor? Sneaked down
from the dry and cracking land, past the roadblocks, past the
Board officials, to make your small home by picking through
rubbish. To live here without papers, taking back-roads from
fear? With upstart kids that make you eat your blackleg shop-
ping till you vomit Omo and chicken from the white super-
market into the sand.

---

* The Kaffir in his place.

Another skirmish in the Third-world War. Keep them down, beat cheap labour down down, the men must work and the women must weep and the cream from the top keeps us soft in our sleep. Enlist the conservatism of tribal culture, torn from the land, from the cattle, to keep them down down. Enlist boys, young boys from country homes, a blue-eyed nation's yearning pride, uniformed, weaponed, junked up in armoured vehicles helicopters fighterplanes, in fatigues with guns handgrenades bullets bombs ... to keep the gold oil manganese iron uranium uranium tea coffee coal chrome copper tin lead pumping pumping in. To keep the computers cheaply assembled, the cars stamped out, stamped out, stamped out, stamped out.

— Three or four thousand homes, thirty thousand lives. The fucking Danes, even bloody twerpy little Denmark, have given more aid than South Africa.

Billy's furious with the particular fury of a man who is caught in the tension of wanting to cry and of being a man, with the pain of the people and the great sloth of his soul. Mr Donothing, the well-known parvenu. He walks up and down the kitchen while Sue sits with the paper.

Up and down. Shout. Don't shout.

— Sue.

— What? Stop being a billiard-ball in there.

— I want to scream.

— So scream. I'll block my ears.

— I can't. I can't even fucking scream.

He stands with his mouth opening and closing like a guppy, plays with the idea of smashing things, of taking all the plates, cups and throwing them.

No, there's been enough, enough breaking.

He walks to where she's sitting and leans over from behind, puts his chin on her shoulder, warm ear touching cold one, starts pounding on the back of her chair in a rhythm. She says:

— I know. At least, I think I do. But try not to turn into a blob of self-pity over it. It almost seems as if you're more upset on your own account than theirs. Look at you.

— That's cheating. That's fucking unfair. Don't look at me, nobody's saying, 'Look at me.' We must look at them, at them, not us.

He bashes the paper with his pointing finger, making a sort of dry rattling noise.

— What can I *do* Suzy, what can we do?

— For you? Or for them?

— For us. I want to do something for all of us.

She breathes out slowly, her eyes closed, folds the paper, puts it down and takes his head curled in her arm, rocks, rocks.

Here's nothing new: old Yeats knew it well, and he a Billy too. All things fall and are built again. The one asbestos sheet that was the back wall by the big bed, bursting like gunfire as the flame winds round and round. Run. Burning.

— When I drove back from Somerset West today, real people, Sue, just standing, standing doing nothing, maybe with some small bundle, or a child. Here, feel it, look! I'm made of flesh, like them, like any carcass hanging in a butcher shop. I thought of Blake how he said that good should be done in minute particulars not general good and I could see could feel that general good, that mad men's planning in some government office or a meeting place, had left them there. Washed up by the wave. I bashed on the steering-wheel with my fist. And the great smoke from the burning. Jesus Jesus Jesus.

She holds his head rocking.

— Well, you've given. Half your clothes, your tent, half my clothes too.

— Aagh! Charity! I want to DO something, to stop it to stop it from happening. It's people, it's humans, it's babies, little babies, Sue. I feel like my life is being torn down the middle. Tomorrow morning I go back to the Creditors' System Interface. Can you even start to *imagine* what my world of work is like?

— Yes. Don't forget that I work too, and my work's probably much more inane than yours. You mustn't always think
that you're so special. Hang on, I think the rice is ready. You
could join. I haven't noticed you being all that active in the
struggle.

— I knew you'd say that. I was waiting for that. I, er. I
can't.... Wait. I don't know how to relate to that. I think, aah
it's unfair. I'm not a joiner. And what about you?

I'm not the only one,
I'm not the only one,
not the only one.

Silence punctuated by clinking cutlery.

*Not a joiner. True, and not true.... The secret image, the
core of my fear. Glenda and I have come back to it again and
again: finding Jessica. Not a joiner, not an organisation man.
Too much self, too many years of Western culture of me
mememe. All the books I've read, all the intelligent conversations, the drugs, the strange seductions in the night's warmth,
all tending on and up to a level of* criticism *that makes everything look cheap and thin, the People's Struggle, all the dull
daft slogans of the boggy massmind, the stupid leaders and the
more stupid followers chanting chanting till it's all filled with
the chant like a trance-mantra and there's no thought. Too
much thought, too hard to give up, give up twenty-nine thousand a year, my house and the Netsuke, I didn't take any of*
those *down to the Red Cross with the heap of clothing
blankets food. Call myself an Anarchist, no rule is good
rule, but not the sly brave Anarchist of the* Attentad, *not
the Syndicalist of the Spanish FAI, Christ, more than a
million paid-up members. Who remembers Makhno?* With
his starving men he took the whole Ukraine in 1921, against*

* Nestor Makhno (1889–1935) was the 'leader' of the Ukrainian anarchist militia around the time of the Russian revolution and civil war. He
was imprisoned by the Czarists between 1908 and 1917. After his release,
the anarchist 'army' was responsible for the liberation of most of the Ukraine between 1919 and 1920 (a feat roughly equivalent to the 'liberation'
of South Africa). The red army under orders from Trotsky was turned on

*superior ordinance? Till Trotsky re-wrote it with bullets in
the night and the black stripe of the censor's pen. I'm not
the hard and gentle Prince Michael Kropotkin, the wise old
Tolstoi, I can see him in hat and net, going to get honey
from the grove of bees. What sort, then, what does this
Anarchist DO? Nothing and nothing again, Mr Donothing.... What about the play about Emma Goldman?
Finished only fifteen penscrawled pages. Unpublished. William, do you work with your hands? Do you take a bucket
down to feed the pigs, swing a pick chanting* Abelungu,
Goddam, Abelungu, Goddam, Abelungu, Goddam, Abelungu, Goddam,* *do you sit in the night, one-light-bulb
room, taking apart an alarm-clock, trying again to make a
bomb that'll work? Carry a malnourished child on your
back down past the deep dongas to where the water runs
thin and dirty in the cracked mud? Do you stand in the
garbage rain watching the bulldozer scuttle swamp smash
demolish the work of your straining arms? William?*

— I don't want to eat.

— It'll do you good.

— I've got a sore tummy.

*What will Glenda say if I tell her I'm leaving my job, leaving
selling going ... where? What will I say? What will Mike say?
'Bill, I'm really disappointed in you, we had high hopes for
you, there was a career waiting for you, there was a real future
here for you.' A real future. Just put a bomb in the front-
office, run, dive rolling down the stairwell feel the heat noise
little bits of microchip shit flying bouncing. All the papers,
burning. All the minutes of meetings, program listings, IRP
forms, leave application forms, timesheets, memos, reminders
reminders, cathode-ray tubes exploding shooting out deadly*

the anarchists in 1921. Makhno fled, and ultimately died in Paris in 1935,
poor and almost friendless. There is no mention of him or the enormous
Ukrainian anarchist movement in Trotsky's *History of the Russian Revolution.*

   * Goddam white man.

rays, boardroom solid-oak table splinters burning burning. Telephone plastic melt droop. Mainframe magnetic-core tape-drive disc-drive, God, the liberated highspeed disks spinning, slicing, rolling through cabinets.

How many times have I tried the combinations on the brief-case? Six, seven? Six seven three four, no, six seven three five, no. Six six six six, number of the great beast, plus one ... no. Feel for the little tumblers to fall, click click. The first one's a four, it's gotto be a four. Four one one one, no. Aatjie, you Bluebeard bastard, what's in here? Pamphlets, papers, gelig-nite? No, not gelignite, not dangerous he ran with it. Dis-kettes, all the paid-up members on one huge mailing list ... or, what? What if they find it? 'Mister Marks, Mister William Knox Marks? Yes. May we come in, Mister Marks, just a routine matter. I believe you're a friend of, er, Aatjie Sep-tember.' Shit. Shitshitshit oh shit. 'We just going to go through the house on the offchance you know. There was a briefcase with important documents.' Never heard of him. Deny deny. 'Dankie, le Roux, sit dit hiersô.[1] *Yours, Marks? What's the combination again? Oh, I see. Gee vir my 'n mes. In die kombuis, doos.'*[2] *Slit, cut it comes open. To show what? Stolen transistor radios? Rare books? The Frans Hals from the Michaelis Collection, sliced from its frame and rolled up cracking? Four one one four, no. Four one one five, no. Shit.*

He straightens up to look at her: her hair smooth and a little bit ruffled where he'd put his head on her shoulder. Her face is blank, her hands lie in her lap without movement, relaxed and lifeless. His vision strobes between seeing her calm and real and seeing an ingenious waxwork, wound up to breathe and blink. Over to the edges of his field of vision, the dark-and-neon shapes of the space behind his closed eyes hum and shift.

— And what are you going to do?

1 Thanks, le Roux. Put it down here.
2 Give me a knife. In the kitchen, twerp.

— It's the same. For me. I don't know. Try to understand, mister *numero uno,* just try. I feel it too.

She stares, pushes her chair back and goes to the window. Opens it, looks out. The rain has started. Light misty Cape winter rain. Coming down indifferently, slanting, blowing spiral in a gust. In at the window onto the sill.

The gentle rain.

You take what you can get and move, what one small person can carry. Burning, burning.

Defending the Mother

14–16 June 1986

— Forget everything. Well, nearly everything. We're off for the weekend! Dirty, I hope. Three whole days!

— Sex isn't dirty. Not with me, I like clean sheets.

— But a weekend with wellies on in the winter mud. That's a dirty weekend for you. Yum. Come tired and sweaty and make love in front of the fire.

— Have you been reading *Playboy* again, you obsessed pornographer?

— Me? Little old me? Why would I want to read *Playboy* with you around?

— Oh you little shit. Is that what I am? A split beaver, huh? Is that it? Centrefold Sue?

— Aah, come on. What's all this hardcore stuff?

— It's me, buddy. I've got a hard core. And you're not taking that bloody computer with you. Please.

— It's one of the few chances I might get for a bit of uninterrupted work. I can limit it to, say, four hours a day.

— Two.

— Hey, unfair! I'm not fighting. We're on holiday, remember.

Which makes the drive out a brooding one. Not that there's nothing else to brood about. That *Weekly Mail* is on the back seat, the one with all the blacked out bits. Elsewhere in the country, behind the barbed-wire entanglements of silence, townships and necklaces burn. They go through two roadblocks, waved whitely on. Monday's the Sixteenth of June. Caroline had said, 'Phew, Bill, you can't go on the N1 this weekend. The roads'll be teeming with blacks.' The roads don't teem, except for the convoys of Casspirs and Buffels, Cape Corps cowboys on scramblers. Billy says:

— Everyone's a bit jumpy these days. In their personal lives, I mean. It's a horrible situation. And the bugger of it is we've always known, more or less, how horrible the things going on about us were. *Ja, during ze recent voar, I vas ein streetsveeper from Hambourg. Of course ve didn't know vot zey vere doing. I just had to do mein job. A men must eat, ja?*

— Have we known, though?

— I have.

They drive the rest of the way in silence.

The cottage is small, with a fireplace and tiny kitchen. There's no electricity but lamps and candles on all the shelves. Quarry-tile floors, high thatch roof. The interior smells of roof-beam creosote, thatch. There's a cat (his real name's Mao, but he's ended up being called Mister Tung) who comes drifting in from the bush, a piece of tabby smoke. The suitcase is brought in and, food unpacked, Sue flops on the bed.

— I think I could like it here. I really could. When I was little I lived under thatch in a big old farmhouse near Worcester. The same *dakriet* thatch as this. My bedroom was an attic, really, with a xylophone wooden staircase going up.

— When I was small I lived under corrugated iron. With a ceiling. When it hailed the noise was like nothing else I've ever heard. Hello Tung you marauding old beast.

— Billy.

— Yeah?

He looks up from the portable word-processor.

— I think … I don't know how to say this. I want to

leave my job, but I'm scared. Bill, if it all goes wrong, if something goes wrong, will you look after me?

She's crumpling her pulled-down sleeve in her hand, looking ahead into the fire. Her book is on the floor, a page folding under its weight.

— Well, I always thought repping was no job for someone with a degree in Anthrop. An honours degree, at that. What are you going to do?

— Look for something else. Something a bit more meaningful. But until then I want to work in one of the relief efforts. Shawco, Red Cross, anything. As a volunteer. Sorting clothes, cooking soup, whatever. I've got enough saved to keep me going for six, seven months. After that I don't know. I don't even know if I care. And I'm going back to the Black Sash.

— You can't go back to the Black Sash. It's probably illegal anyway. Everything is. Since today. And they're all in jail.

— Only one that I've heard of. And even if they were, that'd be a good reason in itself. They *need* all the help, all the people they can get. Now especially.

Mister Tung jumps up onto Billy's lap, settles into a curve, and is still. Billy strokes him — Tung, you sybarite — and looks and looks at Sue. His mind has vacated itself, baled out. He says

— If you live with me you won't have to pay rent. I'll do what I can.

She gets up and comes to hold him. Stupid twist around the upright of the high-backed chair.

— Billy, I'm so scared.

— Me too. I'm just as scared.

— There's going to be such pain. A bloodbath, I can feel it.

The memory, the fear, the fear comes back. *My poor country, Jess, oh Jessica.*

How do you unhug? Pull her close to you, mohair,

human real hair. Pat her back, feel the spine and shoul-
derblades.

— Please. Dont talk about bloodbath. Please. Use
another word, one day I'll tell you, tell you why.

— I'm getting something into shape here. The weapons
people have just returned from doing something out there,
I'm not sure what. Here, have a look.

The printer has just stopped. Zit, Zit, Zit. He tears off
the last page, folds the heap, removes the sprocket holes.

There's something going on. The atmosphere's changed,
there's a feeling of inexplicable excitement about. People
have been arriving, quietly arriving in the night, drifting in
from the fields, a few in the transport truck. There are
new faces in the workshop, in the kitchens. And meetings,
groups of them gathered here and there, talking seriously,
shouting. The business of living went forward as before: I
helped with the wall, which was nearing completion. One
of the new people was helping, a taciturn woman with
huge powerful shoulders.

During the rest after the midday meal, I found Mylia in
her room, lying in the sleeping-hollow with her hands
behind her head. I sat on the floor.

'Mylia, new people have come. I keep seeing people I
haven't seen before.'

'Yes. People have been returning.'

'What's happening? There seems to be a difference,
something new.'

'Old times come back again. Nothing is new.'

'Explain it to me.'

'This is a long explanation. Perhaps you should ask old
Hina. A lot of it is with him.'

She was quiet for a while.

'I haven't met Hina. Who is he?'

'He is a teacher of weapons. He was my first lover,
more than thirty years ago. A hard and gentle man, but

impatient. I'm not sure what he would make of you.'

'And the others. They are soldiers?' I struggled with the word.

'No, Peter. We have no soldiers. They are people of spirit, of heart like you and me. I was a student and teacher of weapons for fourteen years. Then I sat with Mynor and Eenirh to learn the exchanges, the energy pathways. I learn them still.'

She reached out, took my hand and stroked it. Her hands were warm, dry. I could feel calluses.

'So precious, so full of life. And all the way from another world. How does it feel to enter the gateway in the great sphere?'

'I was terrified. Naked. And still bruised from the flight up in the shuttle. It feels like nothing. You close the door and drop into the centre of the sphere. Inside, it's white, too. Brilliant and featureless. Bigger across than the whole village here. You float out to the centre, and, after a certain time, I don't know how long, there are forces that pull you down to the door again. Only, it's the door in the sphere above your world, above Geir. You don't feel the change.'

'I would like to do that. To float bodily in the great white open space.'

'You were telling me about Hina.'

'Ah. Hina goes out time and again to defend the mother. I have been myself, ten, eleven times. Everyone goes. This time there was a strategical error. Someone was caught and we expect that trouble will come from the North.

'I want to sleep now, for an hour. Sleep here with me, if you like.'

She tugged my arm, urging me into the hollow, then rolled over. For the rest of the time I lay with my heart hammering in my chest. The heat of the midday was thick and oppressive. She slept, her breathing deep. After a while she turned, without waking, and held me in her arms. I lay stiff and still, unable to embrace or withdraw, sweating.

— I like it. I don't understand everything in it but it's fine, just fine. One thing, though: you've got to stop feeding me little bits like this. Tell me the whole story. And what's all this stuff about spheres?

— I don't know the whole story yet. You'll have to wait, wait for more to shape itself. The spheres are sort of, I dunno, a way of getting around the faster-than-light problem. I thought of using Ursula Le Guin's universe, lifting it over whole, and just ignoring all that technical stuff, but any SciFi story has to have its hunk of pseudo-science. I haven't written the first part yet, how he gets there. Travels from Earth. But it's up here.

— Ask her another question for me. Will you?

— Sure. What?

— Ask her what to do here in South Africa, now. Will you ask her that?

They move over the little trail between the salty scrub and down to the beach, crunching over the deep layers of shells.

The rocks are orange and gold, old Cape sandstone with patches of lichen. Years, centuries, whole glacial ages of the intricate geometries of temperature, of wind, rain, erosion and pressure have etched the ordered lines of cracks and faults, running into triangulated shadow.

Though the day is clear and calm, the waves, peaking onto the reef, still ripple with the power and height of yesterday's northwester, are green and cream with foam. Gulls make their noises, pursue the interests of gulls. Sea lettuce and anenomes in the rock pools, spikes of a green urchin shell. A crab moves his patch of purple into a crevice. There are stones and shells in the grooves between the round rocks.

Suddenly, across the whole stretch and right up into the brush, a great pattern! The sea-lice march in perfect precision, all going in the same direction, moving in a grey particulate flood. They've scented the warm sliming kelp, and all the rocks right up to where the shore turns at the headland show their ranks, wave on wave in perfect living formation.

— Look, Bill.

— Ooer. Sea lice.

— No, not ooer. They're beautiful. Look. Just at that stretch of rock. Imagine it's an artwork, this piece here, from there to there. The colours! And it moves.

— Do the colours include the sky? I mean, look at that sunlit orange against the blue. It does move. That's quite something. I still find it a bit creepy, to have actual lines in motion like that. Kinetic art. And look at the next rock here. Definitely the same artist.

— Yes, but I think it's later work. The triangular pattern is much more sophisticated. And see how it repeats itself in the smaller bits down there.

— The guy's a creepy-crawly pervert. And here's a dinky handbasin with, hey! a whole little ecology in it! Come and look, starfish.

They're moving over the boulders now, following the artist's phases ... deep sepia, umber, a genuine emerald green. Billy notices that all that the sea-lice want to do is get out of the way.

— Hey, check this, they've got a program which says, 'If you see a large shape looming over you, run forward in a random direction until you hit a crack. If the crack is large enough, hide; else do the bit about random running.' Simple and elegant, really. They're hardwired to be scared of us. I think I'm almost starting to like them.

— D'you think it's the looming shape, I mean do they see us?

Which results in a series of tests, banging on the rocks and shouting. It does seem, in the end, that the looming shape is the stimulus, the scuttle-and-hide the response. *Once you get in a crack, lie still until either a: a fixed time has elapsed or b: the shape in the sky has become absolutely still or moved on. Do they run for clouds?*

All this time Billy and Sue have been following the direction of the sealice, until they are sitting above a groove between sharp high rocks. Down in the gully below is a bed of washed-up kelp, feet deep and turning to slime underneath. In the great web of tangled loops the sea-lice feast, little sand-fleas jump. And Billy finds that the edge-to-edge grey creepy crawly rug of manyfeeted little animals don't produce the usual shivers of revulsion in his back and shoulders, but, jeez, he's getting a hardon! Without a thought of sex in his head!

— Behold the mother of the world! Its weird, but suddenly that mess down there feels *erotic* to me.

— Tell me.

— I don't know. You tell me.

— Well, it's slimy and fecund, but that's on a very primal level.

— Feel it. Erotic is on a primal level, lover.

She looks out beyond into the breathing waves rocking their shiny dolphin selves, feels herself bedded in stone with the great sea her lover, the living shore touching, moving through her body. Not just this gully but all the shoreline right down to the shelf-edge of the deeps is her sex, eating and eaten, making life for life, sweet slime manna for scuttly things, shells and molluscs sucking on her skin warm and cool with the sun, sea, rain. The sensation lasts a moment and when Billy looks at her the tears have come. *Freeze, stare at her.*

— You're right. It is erotic.

She puts her arms around him, rubbing his shoulders, and the sobs start to heave out of her, an almost retching sadness, coming up for breath. On and on while he holds her swaying and looks out at the waves. The sun's road on the water. When they move on, he is wiping his eyes.

A Firm Handshake

16 May 1986

The building is up in the top of town, near Parliament; not big, only five or so stories. It has an already dating Post-Modernist facade plonked over it like icing on a cake and CRENCOR HOUSE, in pillar-box red over the door. Parking's a problem up here.

Down at the entrance there's heavy-duty security. Three blue uniforms hang out at the door, another two at the desk. One of them phones up — Yes he's expecting you. Please come with me and they get into the lift, hit the third-floor button. Endless mirrors reflect Billy, the guard, Billy, the guard. He thinks of the tin on the Royal baking-powder tin on the Royal baking-powder tin.

The reception area: a Delicious Monster in a big round plastic pot, a woman in powder blue, a little sign saying Mej. E. P. du Toit. *Hullo Miss E.*

— Marks. William Marks. Mr van Wijk is expecting me.

— Oh, yees. Mister Marks.

She punches the intercom, speaks in Afrikaans. It growls back at her.

— Will you come through please?

They walk down the corridor, past rows of offices, past the photostat machine humming, with two women hovering near it. Past the coffee, hot chocolate, soup, tea machine. The door has an aluminium sign, ENSEL VAN WIJK. She knocks lightly, deferentially. — *Kom binne.*

— Ja, Mister Marks. *Dankie, skat.* Won't you have a seat.

The man's face is beautiful: an old angel's face from a Quattrocento painting, high and firm, late forties. He has grey hair, slightly balding and he's wearing a pearl-grey *what looks like, yes it is, a* silk suit, three-piece. A cufflink with a very yellow diamond peers out of a sleeve. There's a grey diagonal tie and his smile shows crooked teeth at the top. They shake hands over the desk, a massive plateau of rosewood veneer.

— Well, Mister Marks, so you work with MacFarlaine, hey? He tells me that you're the best in town. — He laughs. — But we're all the best in town aren't we? Otherwise we wouldn't get anywhere.... Ja, here at Crencor we, how shall I say, we put a high premium on excellence. We value drive and discipline.

He touches his fingertips together slowly and precisely.

— Mister Marks, what do you know about front-end security? Sign-on protection, all that sort of thing?

— I wrote almost nothing else at Anglo for a while. But doesn't the operating system take care of all that nowadays?

— The operating system. Of course. And then there's all the libraries of utilities.

He gestures at a shelf of manuals, gets a file out of the drawer and places it in front of him, squared on the empty desk.

— But we're really looking for something more, well, non-standard. Something that would be more, ah, immune. You know, our system is on networks, and we can't really have just anyone violating confidentiality. There's a lot of these young kids out there man, hackers, kids that know their way around the operating systems, that have cracked the utilities long ago. What MacFarlaine was going to do for us, what you could do for us is actually a standard procedure here. We contract someone outside of our Data Processing department, you know, to re-write the security front-end.

Every six or eight months. It's a little informal standard we have. I don't need to explain why, do I? We're both, er, men of the world, aren't we? There's a lot of, er, of privileged information on our systems. Participation bonds, share portfolios, that sort of thing. And our keyword here at Crencor is confidentiality. Security. We expect you to plug it so tight that even you yourself can't get in. Not without the passwords, which we'll be changing, oh yes.

— Yes, I understand. I feel sure that I could come up with something.

— Of course. But would it be something new? A unique protection that won't fall apart the first time someone fiddles with it? Not that we really expect fiddlers, but you know, these days a man just can't be too cautious. And caution is where the dividends lie. Caution combined with a bold approach, that's good generalship. That's what our country needs.

— Well, I'll certainly give it my best.

— Yes, yes. I'm sure of that.... And of course, the reimbursement, the pay, will be excellent. Pay a good man for a good job done, that's what I always say. We're looking at, let's see, say eight nights of work, more or less three to four hours a night. Let's say thirty-two hours over two or three weeks. — He gets out his calculator. — That would make two thousand four hundred. Make it a round two five. How does that sound to you, hey?

— That sounds really fair, Mister van Wijk. I could use it.

— So could we all. A flat rate, no penalty clauses, if you come in under the time, the money's yours anyway. MacFarlaine has done it for us before, you know. And my experts here have assured me that he did a next-to-perfect job. So, if we've got his recommendation to go on, then I have a lot of confidence in you. A lot of confidence.

No, he doesn't know that Dave's done anything for them. *Which means that Dave was bullshitting when he said he didn't have the details. And there'll be a whole lot of forms to*

*sign, full of fine print. They'll say: 'Shut up or we take you to
the cleaners.' And, yes, he's opening that file and here comes
the first one.*

— Are we agreed then? Let's say it's done, let's shake
on it, Mister Marks. That is with a K, hey? Like Full
Marks. You do understand that officially this has never
happened, we never had this little talk. And I must em-
phasise that we don't want a lot of loose chatter, especially
in the DP world. Can't have our boffins up in Jo'burg
asking why there's been an outsider brought in over their
heads, now can we? Well, if you can just fill in this lot, all
the places where you see the little pencil ticks, and sign
next to the x'es. Ja. And you can let Eeufeesia help you if
there's any problem. You have your ID book on you?
Good. Then we can sign and witness them and the deal is
made. I like to act fast here. I like to think that I'm not a
man to go for a lot of red tape, hey? Your first briefing
will be on the, ah, twenty-second of June. Six p.m. A few
things have come up, there are always these little delays,
aren't there? Have you got that? Good. Gives you a bit of
time to think about what you're going to do, hey? And
thank you sir.

He leans over to the intercom — *Skattie, kom help gou
vir Meneer Marks met die forms** — gets up, comes around
the desk and shows Billy to the door. A firm handshake, a
smile — So nice meeting you — and they go down the corridor again with her, to sign the forms.

*It does make a sort of paranoid sense, to get an outsider to tie
in the security routines, doesn't it? Then of course you take
him off into the countryside and make him dig a big hole, six
foot. Men standing around in balaclavas and toting machine
guns as the red earth piles on the green grass. Or cement
shoes, over to the container basin, down to Davy Jones's
Locker. Cheers.*

---

* Help Mister Marks with the forms please, dear.

He looks at the two-hundred-and-fifty-buck *advance*. It has two indecipherable signatures. One of them could be Cilliers, or maybe Viviers. The other one's a series of blue ink swirls with a line shooting off to the right. *pp CRENCOR*. The company number is at the bottom of the cheque, stamped in by Miss du Toit at the last minute, in purple ink. *A blank cheque till van Wijk had filled in W. K. Marks and the amount. Oh for a few of those blank cheques.*

— Ten per cent on signing, Mister Marks. I forgot to mention it.

Two side-clips click undone and the screen slides up and forward. Now unhitch the keyboard from the back, plug it in, twiddle the plug until the kink slides into the groove. Good. Now for the mains. Get the cable from the top drawer, push it in at the back, find the extension lead, down behind the desk. Get onto your hands and knees, hook the power cable down over the back. *Zap in she goes. He goes.*

He sits down, shuffles the upright wooden chair into place. Switch on. Thirty seconds for a memory check. He can see over the top of the screen to the bookshelf with a little bronze Nepali Buddha, a skinny one. There's a feather standing in a bottle like in Struwwelpeter, Tall Agrippa's great goose-feather in the inkstand that had frightened him when he was six.

Gnink eeep! The screen lights up. He hits the enter button reflexly twice, types WP for word processing. To add a few more bricks to the wall that keeps the barbarians out, shoring up the walls of consciousness. To keep the sense of the wildly gyrating *real* out.

Now for the Turkish Bath scene. Lemme think, he's in the steam-room and

We sit in the steam-room, sweating, twelve or thirteen of us. Night has come outside, the unfamiliar night. People are discarding the day's work from muscles and bones. My body

*looks pink, albino, in among all the dark gleaming skin.
Sweat runs into my beard, eyes. No-one pays any special attention to me.*

*Mylia comes in, I can make her out through the steam. She
looks around and spots someone, diagonally across the room
from me. She sits next to her and they embrace, wet and
misty. I stare at her, the first time I've seen her naked. The
two of them sit and hold hands, talking in a low voice. I catch
a few words blurred by the steam. '... towards the stand of
trees, then he also arrived and ...', or: '... they didn't see her.
She was behind th ...', sinking back into mutters. I am fas-
cinated by her body. Thick like a tree, with almost no waist
at all. Brown. There are folds where her trunk meets her
thighs, and her breasts are small and collapsed, flattened on
the top.*

*The wooden beams of the room have been stained in pat-
terns of green and blue. Pegged together, without nails or
screws. The carpenters here must measure well.*

*When I can bear it no longer, I get up and go to where she
is, sit on the other side of her. She puts her hand on my knee
and squeezes, an acknowledgement. '... and old Teshu's
uncle, the one with the gammy leg, he helped her to open
them. Some funny trick with a knife, he does it so easily.'
The other woman snorted. 'Old Teshu's uncle, how old do
you think he is? Seventy, seventy-five? I happen to know
that he's hardly more than sixty-six. Still thinks he's a gym-
nast in bed, I'm told.'*

*Mylia says: 'I'll have to seek him out. I have a few spine-
twists of my own, and we must hand the knowledge on.' And
their laughter fills up the little room. Big damp laughter.*

*The other spots me: 'You must be the man from beyond
the sky. Everyone's been talking about you. You've been
down in the pattern-shop printing cloth.'*

*'Yes. Discovering my own clumsiness. I spilt dye onto the
floor.' I show them my leg and foot, spattered with blue.*

Mylia says, 'He wants to ask me questions again. He's got

*more questions in him than the room's got steam. Peter, you
can have one question, then we enjoy the heat. Think of the
questions we could ask him ... a whole world he comes from.
All day long his mind is going round and round like a water-
wheel, but faster. Thinking up questions to ask. I'm still
waiting for the river to run a little drier, to drop just below
the level of his silly turning.'*

*'I was thinking about my own history. My own world. I
wanted to compare a few things, to ask you what you
thought.'*

'Only one.'

*'Imagine a situation where the balance was so badly upset
that, well, property came before people. That an ideology of
possession was put first, I suppose almost like some sort of
god. I'm not speaking hypothetically, I'm speaking out of our
history, out of our present, sometimes.'*

*'You'll have to be a little clearer. About the particulars of
the situation. But yes, the general form is quite familiar. It's
really the most common one in the history of our world, too.
We have only the thirty-two little islands where we keep the
balance. Where we try to keep it, failing and correcting our-
selves all the time. Every time someone calls a challenge,
every time that we have to come back and look at the middle
way, then we know that we've lapsed again into the old
worlds of oppression and submission, however slightly, however finely.'*

*'But on my world, on Earth, there's simply no little island
of balance. Imagine yourself in a place like that. You were
born here, brought up here.'*

*'In a while you must come outside with me. There's some-
thing I want to show you.' She closed her eyes and leant back
onto the wooden wall. Lightly touching the fingers of the
other woman's hand.*

*Outside, the two moons were near each other by now, and
both almost full, making double-edged shadows. I walked
with her down the path, through the food gardens and on to*

the first of the orchards where high firm nut-trees stand, their leaves glossy and dark. We moved on until we were in the middle of the grove, surrounded by the trees. The sound of the leaves in the light wind remains with me.

'Look at the trees. Let your eyes settle and just look at them.' Trees. Big dark shapes. I stood still, until I was aware of the shapes, the presences of the trees.

'Now imagine that a fire comes. Some fool drops a coal, or lightning strikes, or whatever causes trees to burn. Imagine the flames, great big flames. Feel the heat of them on your skin. Hotter than the steam bath, much hotter. Where has the fire come from?'

'From the coal, the one that someone dropped.'

'That's how it started, yes. But if you drop a coal onto a bare rock, nothing happens. Where do the trees get all that heat, that fire?'

'Er ... from the sun?'

'Yes, naturally. From the sun. But imagine a seed, one that's going to grow into a tree. It's in deep space, in isolation, and the sun shines on it. Will it turn the sunlight into a tree, into fire?'

'I think I'm getting the picture.'

'Now look at the trees again. Just ordinary trees. Where is the fire now? Inside them. It is them. Latent fire, energy. Imagine the movement of that fire through time. How carefully the mother guards, treasures and guides that flame, organises it into complexity, into the earth, the air, into you and me. The fire is in you. Dried out, you'd blaze with a fine light. This is the seed of the father.'

I picture that glowing energy held in the form of the trees. And outward, into the world. I see the whole of this world as a fine web of shining lines of fire, piercing through the land, the seas, the sky, winding round us and through us.

... and the thing that happens while he writes is that Mylia goes quietly on her own path, refuses to be *written*, to say the things that he'd wanted her to say. That whole scene has done it. It was all supposed to take place in the Turkish Bath, and Peter was going to wheedle an entire lecture out of her, on the subject of Oppression and Equality. Then he'd have Peter spring the trick question: What would *you* do in a situation like South Africa in 1986? But here they are outside in — what? — a nut orchard, and he's feeling the fine threads of the sun's fire being passed up and down the food chains.

... and that lapse into pseudopoetic at the end there, would he really do that? Yes, in that situation, he might.

Going to have to change, alter a lot. But Mylia will go her own quiet way. The prospect of editing becomes rather like altering the course of a river, using only a spade. A lot can be done with a spade.

Dear Mom

6 June 1986

The duvet makes a tent over Sue's knees, and on her lap there's a copy of *Impressionism and Post-Impressionism* to be used as a writing surface. Billy is reading next to her and drifting between waking and sleep, adjusting the book and deliberately turning pages every now and again, then letting the book fold around his thumb as his eyes droop closed.

She sips cocoa from a mug, catches the skin on a fingertip and lowers it onto her tongue, puts the mug down, sucks her pen and looks out over the linen landscape of swooping blue swallows, squares up the notepaper and begins:

Dear Mom,

First off, let me make the usual excuses about not writing for so long. I've been terribly busy, which is to say that I've been so involved in doing things that I haven't been giving proper attention to some of the basics. Like writing letters or cooking breakfast. (I've been making up by eating *huge* lunches, very unhealthy.) I know that you'll forgive me (after all, that's what mothers are for) and I shall try to write more often. Six weeks, I think it's been.

I'll have to tell her what I've been doing…. No, I won't tell her. She doesn't really want to know, only that her little girl is — is what? — is happy, is growing up to be like her. That's a pretty huge double-bind of its own.

First of all, let me put your fears to rest. Things aren't
as bad as they may look in the press or on your TV. Not
around here, anyway. And we don't see or read anything, because it's all controlled by this awful Information Bureau. But life seems to go on, which feels
absurd, like drinking tea in the sun or having a bath
while a close friend is going crazy in the next room.
Mom, I know that sounds awful, and it is. But honestly,
we're all fine, and I don't feel personally threatened at
all.

*Except every time I read the papers. Or don't read them. Or
look at the news. Or write a letter like this where you have to
lie to — to what? — to make her happy? to tell the 'truth' she
wants to hear? Can she hear my lies? Mom I don't feel personally threatened at all, Mom life is perfectly normal, Mom just
ignore the news, just ignore our history here and pretend that
your little girl is happily in Montreal or Vancouver having a
romantic affair with the* right *man who's going to marry her
little girl in the spring, when would the spring be, March,
that's what, nine or ten months, it wouldn't be a shotgun.
What could I tell her about Billy? Mom I met this romantic
schmuck, Mom he's* Jewish *but he's blond so that's all right,
and he's a fucked-up neurotic like your little girl, Mom. Mom,
we actually speak to each other and do* things *in bed together,
things I can't even start to imagine you and Dad doing, nice
friendly things. While everything else is on fire, while the
police came to fetch Jake and Patsy and Bruce, we were
touching* each other.... *Oh shit, he's asleep. What can I tell
her about? About work, which is the same except that I'm
leaving it soon. Soon. No, Mom, the boss hasn't made a
pass at me, I'd kick his pudgy shins if he did. Anyway he's
married, talks about Maureen and the kids. What have I
been so busy with?*

I've been seeing a really delightful man, his name's Billy
Marks. He's a Computer Systems Analyst with a big
firm in town (Datlin Consultancy). Although he's fairly

highly placed there, he doesn't seem like a *business man* at all, more like an old friend. We actually seem to be able to *talk* to each other, which is a big attraction after Alvin. Of course, we do argue a fair bit, but I think that's the natural way that adults make space around each other, and there don't seem to be any serious grudges held over. He has a lovely romantic streak, which suits me just fine. He buys flowers and looks so attentively at you when you talk that he makes you feel cared for and thought about. Important. At my age it feels almost girlish to be excited about something like this, but I am. So that's the big event! And just in case you get any thoughts in that naughty mother's mind of yours, there's *no talk* of marriage or anything like that. I wouldn't want there to be, and certainly not yet anyway.

Hm, how did I get there? I suppose Mom's constant Market Awareness seeps in. Hello Mom, the schmuck I'm not going to marry is fast asleep now and his book's fallen off the bed with a thump that didn't even stir him. He's got the most hairless chest I can remember, which is nice for kissing.

She pulls the covers up over him and turns off his reading light, leaning over him carefully so as not to touch. There's still a little cocoa, which she finishes with a shlurping sound, tipping the mug up on her nose.

Billy's a writer, when he's not fiddling with his computers, and he's busy on a long and complicated book. I suppose it's a Science Fiction book, a Utopia of sorts. He has been reading me bits, and though I often don't know how to respond (it seems that you have to learn a whole *language* before you can really appreciate the stuff) it's quite exciting to be that involved.

Enough about all that, I'll tell about Ellen and Dave.

I bumped into Ellen and Dave in the street the other day. Ellen is pregnant! It's going to be a Christmas Baby like me, which lets Auntie Sue off from having to remember another birthday. They were thinking of having it at home, but the doctor won't hear of it. It must be such a dilemma, choosing between those really hostile hospital wards and the less than perfect medical attention one might get with a home birth.

Is she really interested in all this? Yes, but mainly because her baby's writing it to her.

She makes a curled motion with her arm ... *my baby* ... and looks down with affection towards the empty space between the crook of her arm and her breast. A wave of body heat comes up from the bedclothes. Billy's turned over and his back is sweaty against her hip.

Ellen *promised* she'd write to you and took your new address in Ottawa and everything, so you can expect to hear from them fairly soon. Her head-girl streak makes her very diligent, unlike your wicked daughter.

Last weekend I put down a variety of bulbs in pots on the balcony, freesias and some local wild lilies whose names I forget. Alium something, I think. The jasmine didn't make it through the winter: there have been some huge north winds and one of them tore it off the wall and rolled the pot around on the balcony all night. I console myself by thinking that it was suffering from neglect anyway, and I'll get a new one in the spring.

Have I thanked you for your lovely long letter? No, I see I haven't. I was really sorry to hear about Emily and all her tribulations.

Sorry to have to slide my eyes over those parts, who the hell is Emily anyway? Where did I put her letter?

She slides out of bed, grabs the shawl that's draped over a chair and wraps it around her ... *It must be in the second drawer* ... and pads through to the spare room. *Hm, yes. God, twelve pages and all neatly typed.* Billy's voice comes from the bedroom:

— What you doing?

— Just fetching something. Go back to sleep.

— Wasn't sleeping. I was thinking.

She comes back into the bedroom with the letter. He's propped up on his elbows, his eyes all screwed up. His light is on again and backlights his face with a curly halo.

— Still writing to your mom?

— Yes. And what have you been thinking, O sage?

— Unh. Come here. I want to make a trumpet noise in your navel.

— Oho. Jericho watch out.

She shivers and pulls the cover up. His head dives under and there is a period of kicking and squealing.

— That *tickles!* It's your hair. Stop it, no, no!

He's got her T-shirt pulled up and shivers his hair up and down her body making whooping noises while she writhes and hesitates between defending herself and going with the stabbing ticklefinger for the certain vulnerability of his side, between the hip and the ribs. Finally she connects both sides, digs in mercilessly. In moments she's sitting on him and he's a blubbering heap of tearful giggling helplessness.

— Give up?

— Yes memsahib. Please. Aagh! No no Nanette!

— No no who?

— No no Sue. You. Nanette was prelapsarian. Aah, stopit.

— I'm going to finish my letter. Then we'll deal with the Nanette question.

— *Ja Merrem. Ja my Sieur, my Koning.*

Mom, I was so pleased to read that you want to come out at the end of the year. What's it been now, almost eighteen months. Of *course* you can stay with me, if you want to. I've got the spare room all set up and waiting. I do think, though, that you'll be so much more comfortable with Annie than in my poky little flat, but why don't you think about doing a sort of time-share and moving from the one to the other? And don't worry about our crazy politics affecting you, just come. As I

said, the areas you'll be staying in are almost totally un-
affected by anything. The rich are so strong.

*Don't think I should have said that, but it'll look even
sillier if I cross it out. Or more sinister. And I'm not re-writing
the page.*

— Where you going?

— Get some water. Want anything from the kitchen?

— Yes, bring me a plum from the fridge.

— I ate them. And the red chickens glazed with rain.

— Boo! Sssssss.

On Sunday we (that's Ralph, Alison, Billy and I) went
for a walk along the top of the Twelve Apostles, right to
the point where you can see above Hout Bay. The wind
was bitterly cold and I got sore ears from it. The sun
kept coming out and going back behind clouds and
changing the view. We watched the rain moving in over
the sea and had to go down as huge mist banks started
to gather on the slopes. By the time we got home it was
torrenting down and we got wet just running from the
car to the front door!

That's about it for now. It's twelve forty-five (a.m.)
and I'm getting atrociously sleepy. Look after yourself
and for God's sake get someone else to do the heavy
work around the garden.

With all my love (and hugs to all the others)

O X O X O X O X O X O X

SUE

Billy comes back walking crabwise to hide the peacock's
side-feather he's fetched from the hall just as she's putting
the writing stuff aside and switching out her light. He rolls
over onto his side facing her and says

— G'night. Gimme a kiss.

— Good night love.

About a minute after they're settled in, the feather
inches its way over from behind him to find her ear.

To Remember Auntie Meg

17 November 1972

— Come on, Jess. Come.

— No, you go. I've got work to do.

— More marking. Naah, staircase them. The ones that land on the top stairs get top marks. It gives a better distribution curve, if you get the throw right.

— That may be so, but you lot just fuck right off and leave me to do my work.

Vaughn can see that she's looking down but whatthehell, orders are orders and he's so used to getting her to tell him what to do that he and Billy and Aatjie leave without thinking. Besides he's starting to feel the first little rushes of the half cap he's taken: *California Sunshine, no fooling my buddy this is the real stuff, American Bruce brought it in, stuffed into the hollow frame of his rucksack, fifty caps. Let's see now, street value here two hundred and fifty rands, that's food and shelter for two months at least....*

Clarity: Vaughn's clarity which isn't hallucination, no the world looks ordinary everything in its place: Jessica there at the desk, Billy and Aatjie starting to move with him, *clarity of the hundred thousand million billion trillion electron zing particles all arranged in the order of things. Clarity of the soles of feet bare on the hallway rug feeling into old dusty pile, feeling through the floor into the boards, down into the hollow ratty underworld. Clarity of the light in the door stained glass, no not running, not turning into custard-pudding-cheese but simple real light all the way from the sun, died into the earth, pumped out again as oilburnt electric incandescent streetlamp. The doorhandle, brass, turn it, opening a doorway to the shining street.*

The door closes and Jessica's alone with herself and the big house and the pile of dull essays. Nothing changes.

Alone anyway with myself; and Vaughn and Billy. And Arn upstairs screwing crying out, with the kitchen and vomit-smelling lavatory, with all the facemasks on the walls and the rotting sculptures, alone with the four dimensions of the world pressing on the skull. Leave Mother at home: she'll look after the house, she'll *tidy the lounge and clean the shit off your walls. Leave Mother at home to earn the bread marking fuckenrubbish essays from the first-year class.* The nervous system is composed of the sympathetic and parasympathetic nervous systems. These, in order, control the voluntary and autonomic functions. *CRAP!! CRAP!! CRAP!! CRAP!!.*

Get up. walk downstairs. Vaughn's own face leans out at you on the landing, painted with chevron roadstripes.

Roaded with Chevrolet paintstripes. Here the stairs turn, turn with them, spiral down, past the window to the courtyard and the night through the sitting-room. *The Chesterfield suite, it's stuffed like gross fat tramps in greasy overcoats.* Turn off the amp, turn off the lights, they've left them all to burn again, go through the kitchen, out the back.

Stand in the courtyard, feel the air, pick up the old and dirty bottleneck, throw it away. Pick up papers that the wind has blown, pick up Vaughn's paperback, and feel the air that moves across your face and hands. The air! The kitchen air is sour, from old food. Make table space. Move the dishes one by one out of the sink. The knives and forks go in the jug. Pile the plates up there, the saucers there, and any food you come across, the jam, the butter, put it in the fridge, the Marmite on the shelf. Keep moving, put the cups into the sink. Only cups and glasses. Run the hot. *Oh, there's no detergent.* Get the soap from the bathroom. It's up the stairs again past his chevron sleeping face, eyes closed.

Now go down again and run for the sink before it over-flows. Now wash them one by one and stack them in the rack, the water's hot on your hands. There's a pair of surgical gloves with holes in them hanging limply over the tap. *Old french-letters or strange sea-growths.* The rack gets full. Dry. Run another sink. Start with the plates and scrape the muck into that plastic carry-bag. Wash, stack. *Fingertips are getting wrinkled as the skin expands. Don't think of anything but the next plate, nothing and nothing again. Don't think of Vaughn tripping,* don't think, put the plates away. They rattle into the cupboard. *Not of students, stupid Professor Wilkens, not of mom sitting at home by the electric fire even on the hottest day, of Fuad-Fuadjie-Aatjie and his family, now in some dingy flat on the second floor in Manenberg who used to live in Jarvis Street, next to the merchant, next to where the hippy dippy scum read Tolkien with a stolen church candle in a darkened upstairs room. The rats live well in the shadow of The Group, of eviction notices, police, the Board, the vans, smash them down down down don't think Shut UP!* Do the pots now; scrape muck again. *Arn arsehole making buck-wheat porridge so thick it would choke a bull, no-one ate it not even him.* Scrape it out with a spoon, get a new bag.

Until the room is cleaner than it's been for four full weeks. Don't stop now, the rest of the house is waiting.

Two and one quarter hours gone. No marking. No auto-nomic, nervous, system. No stopping for cupoftea sitdown no stopping the reeling dance of the mind no no no.

Bath now. Bath. Mommy used to bath me rub me with a loofah, till my skin's all tingly, Tanguely, Yves Tanguy.... This is the house of Yves Tanguy, with the what? With the sawmill. This is the house of Yves Tanguy, of poor little me, with the crazy crazy maybe saveme, with the fountain so deep you can hardly fathom, with the talking runs on to the moun-tain mountain. Lion Said, Devil Speak, mountain. This is the house of my bath. I used to play in the yard with Glynnis, with

Arlene, we'd line up stones in little lines to be houses and visit each other and have tea, tea. Showed Tony how girls wee and he cried and ran to his Catholic mother and Daddy hit me and said never never show boys your wee. Hit. Me. Hit.

Bath. Foam bath. Aphrodite bath. Old bathroom, who made thee? What human hands hands laid these Queen Victoria tiles, put the lion's claws on the deep iron, who ... aah. Soap. Damn it, the soap's still down with the dishes, no more dishes. Out; are there ghosts? Of old carpenters and tilers putting the tiles down, one beige one red in diamonds and pale green up the walls. Are they watching me? Look Ghosts, look, see my wee. My foam body.

Out of the bath, towel, dripping, running. Water collects in the crevices. Run down the stairs, Vaughn's grinning now, and look, there's Billy's face with a crown of thorns, real Christ Thorns. Christ, thorns! Ow. Get the soap. Past the tramps, old leering tramps. Up the stairs boom boom boom boom look, footprints: our, my woman Friday. Singing now:

Friday, Friday, Friday clean the house.

Friday, Friday, Friday clean the house.

Razor. Get the razor. Soap legs soapy run hands up feel stubble dark hair, run the razor. Scrape rinse soap rub feel. I'll shave everything, look, It's ME. Mirror mirror on the wall, mirror mirror when you fall, will you hold a million me's? Did he who made the lamb make me shave my dark curly folds? Hook legs over cold rim and ease upwards open my legs my flower, pull the skin, funny bumpy skin. Different colour on this side, that's part of my inside on the outside. He to get the warm side inside put the cold side skin side outside, put the warm side fur side inside turned the whole thing inside outside. Soap rinse scrape soap rinse scrape — Ow, a little blood, ow ow ow. Soap foam. New blade more hot. Hot. Now the top bit. Mound of Venus. Mound of morning star. That's Lucifer, angel of the morning, Just call me angel, of the morning, darling. Just kiss my ... kiss my what? Soap rinse scrape, the bath's full of my hair, nearly done. Look

ghosts. You over there, put down your paintbrush, look. You.
The mound of the morning star, naked and hairless. Bald
balled. Bared for your delight, never to be seen again. Net
through the bath, the foam, harvest the dark hair on my hand.
Drop it wet onto the floor, onto a pale tile. Mirror mirror
who's got the barest one of all? More hot, up to the top of the
overflow. Hot hot hot. Arms, forearms. Left one's easy, all
off, all off now. Everyone off, this is the last stop. Right more
difficult, hold the razor still and move the arm. All off.

Hair, my long hair, my redhenna hair, my Gehenna hair.
Out of the bath no towel, get the scissors in the bedroom. A
tidy bedroom. Back to the steamy long wall mirror. Cut, big
pieces, drop them on the floor. The back's the hardest, look,
there's blood running on my leg, it's up to my ankle. On my
leg. Cut, the special sound of hair in scissors. More, get close
in over the neck, down over the ridges of skull. Back into the
bath, more hot.

Shave. Another new blade. Shave you're a Jew, a prisoner,
you're lousy with lice shave. Soap scrape rinse. Neck forward
the back for parts, shave the back parts, soft curly parts,
there's a little blood now didn't even feel the

   Little blood
   little blood
   didn't even feel
   the little blood

Soap rinse scrape. All gone now. Where's the baby?
There's *the baby. All gone now. Armpits, I've done my*
legpit. Right one always hard. All gone. Clean as a whistle.
Clean as the driven snow. Pure as the Virgin. Dive under,
rinse. Net through the bath, the foam, harvest the dark hair
on my hand.

More hot, hotter. God it's nearly full. Remember mommy
in the bath, sinking down and breathing out, with her
plastic bath cap on and all the white gunk on her face.
Floating, the lady of Shalott, the lady of leek, of spring
onion garlic chives thyme thyme sage old time, sixteen-year-

old again. Where's the baby? There's *the baby. All gone now.*

Now the wrists, new blade, that's the whatsit, fourth? Down into the skin, under the skin. That's my insides, on the outside now. Nick into the tendon Ow Ow Ow Ow OW. Mommy. The other one blood blood look mommy mommy under the water, ah not sore now not sore now, look red foam on the bath, Aphrodite morningstar foam. Feel my wee, there's blood running in my wee, aah relax not sore now.

I remember Daddy with khaki trousers and Roger doggy Roger. Poor old Labrador Roger whose middle ear was broken, infected so that he could only see the world go spinning round, dizzy like a Dervish, whirling Dervish, and he'd tilt his head to make it all seem straight and so he always looked as if he were asking a question.

And I remember Auntie Meg, she's dead. *I'd go to her on Sunday afternoons and walk in her clipped garden with the hedge of boxwood and the bent figtree, broken by a midnight winter gale. She spoke such perfect English, had a Siamese cat called Ming who only ate the best topside, braised in tinfoil, and she cooked roast chicken and risotto, and prepared the camping-bed, which squeaked, for long weekends.*

She bought me toys, dolls and picture-books, and though I was fourteen and had full breasts, I played with them to please her. And we'd walk in her garden, talking about how the roses needed pruning, and drink tea and eat the little biscuits scented like cheap sweets. I would sit with my legs crossed, a young lady. She in her two-piece suit of light linen, and the golden chain with the locket always round her neck.

Aunt Meg, I never asked you what was in the secret golden darkness of that little box that knew your skin and clothes, and shone polished from rubbing lightly on your cream silk blouse.

*You were my mother's cousin, the spinster one, but ru-
moured in the family to have had (when you were twenty-
five or so) a wild and difficult affair. He left, to die in the
minefields at Tobruk, or in some dark and hungry Polish
concentration camp.*

*I remember Auntie Meg, the winter sun finding highlights
in your greying auburn hair, walking with me in Kirsten-
bosch and showing me how this small grey mountain herb,
when crushed, would give a dark and sweet and bitter scent.
All day that smell was covering my hands, secret invisible
gloves, that you and I and no-one else could feel.*

*Mozart and Chopin in the living-room from the polished
rosewood hi-fi set. Only the simple pieces, only those which
were sad and unaccompanied. Once from your big heavy
box auntie, old scratchy seventy-eights, the Bach partitas,
savoured one at a time like expensive chocs.*

*And when the sun had gone behind the mountain, when
the cold crept in from under the leaves on the shaded lawn,
I'd get dressed in my Sunday clothes: stockings, straw hat
and grey school dress. Every time I'd want to cry, but I'd
look brave and put the toys away and pack my things. My
poor dead aunty Meg, do they let you wear your locket
there? With the long green grass rooting in your soul. soul,
growing all over you.*

...not sore now not sore ... not ... poor old Roger.

Ophelia in Red

9 June 1986

He sits looking at Glenda, winding himself up to tell her. To say it.

— It was at Onrust with Sue. I got it back, the whole thing. It lasted perhaps two or three seconds, I mean remembering. God it's so hard....

— And you want to look at it now.

— No. I never want to look at it. Never wanted to.

A silence again. Glenda sits calm and still in her big blue grandpa chair.

Do you shit, sphinxwoman? If I cut you will you bleed, or will the android parts, little wires and cables, transistors resistors, Christ resistors! Wouldn't you like to know? Glenda, there's a briefcase in my cupboard, full of the worms and maggots of my past. Lying there like a dead cow. Dead with the flies buzzing out of it. Glenda there's a briefcase with Dad dying and Jessica shaved dead in her bath. With Mr van Jaarsveld caning my little nine-year-old bum, one two three four in the pipesmoke-smelling office. Bite lip hold mouth closed — Dankie Meneer *— run for the door....*

— Will it make a difference? If I tell you?

— That's up to you. You know that.

— Okay, I'll try. Uh … it must have been about four in the morning. We got back home, me and Cheryl and Vaughn and Aatjie. Back from the club, we'd been stoned, Vaughn was tripping. Well, he was … I don't know … coming down.

His hands are clenching and he's hunched over, looking at the pattern on the Persian rug. Not seeing it.

— I can't ... go on.

He's rubbing his trousers now, swaying backwards and forwards, rubbing.

— Try. What happened at Onrust, to make you remember?

— I don't know. It was something Sue said. Bloodbath. She said there's going to be a bloodbath.

— And that was Jessica?

— You knew her. What do you remember about her? She taught you.

— Yes, but only a few seminars. She arrived in my last year and we did something on Laing. The more radical students loved her. She was on their side.

— And you? Did you love her too? I'm skiving again, aren't I?

— Yes I think you are. But we can go as slowly as you like.

— I was the one. I saw her first, walked into the bathroom first. It was horrible, it was just horrible. I can't ... I walk into the bathroom, I'm tired, so tired, from dancing all night. When we got in, creeping in quiet so as not to wake anyone, shit, the house was *tidy*. Pangs of guilt, she's done it again. Even the kitchen floor was washed. We went to the kitchen to make tea. I remember, it was Oolong tea that Arn had bought, funny how these stupid details come up. We sat around the table, and Arn fussed in his usual way: you know ... the teapot must be warmed.... Fuad, oh, that's Aatjie, and Vaughn, he was Jessica's lover, they put in milk and sugar. And Arnold gave them his little lecture. About tea and the Tao. And then I went upstairs for a pee.

— Really, Glenda, this must sound so ... trivial. But as I talk, I seem to remember other things and it all gets denser and denser. I, anyway ... Cheryl was there, and I was holding her hand, sort of playing with her fingers like this. All the talking was hardly more than a whisper because of *her* sleeping upstairs. Mm, how can I say ... I don't think you ... er, or anyone could understand, really, how much we loved her. How we whispered, kept quiet for her.... The house could get pretty loud and no-one cared much about anyone else sleeping. But we'd keep quiet for her, if she asked, if she wasn't razzling with us.

— But you wouldn't wash the dishes for her.

Oops, gut blow! But washing dishes was something else, washing dishes and cleaning-the-house were parents' work, *were from that world, and we were in this world and it was spring. Shit, she died in the spring.*

— No, but I'd cook for her. It's true. I liked cooking and I probably ended up doing most of it. But when I cooked, even if they were all my friends, even if Cheryl was there, I was thinking, I was thinking, 'I wonder if *she'll* like this, I'll make bread pudding, I know *she* loves bread pudding.' And I'd buy her chocolates for a treat. The individually wrapped round ones that come in a sort of tube. Those were the ones she liked.

— You went upstairs for a pee.

— Yes, the whole house was tidy. Well, as tidy as it could ever get, I mean, she hadn't dusted the wainscot or anything. But put things away, emptied the ashtrays and wiped them. I was feeling really guilty. I used to promise her I'd clean things up but hardly ever seemed to get round to it.

— I'm coming to the bit about her, just let me get there. I walk up the stairs. Big wide wooden staircase with a turn in it. Not a narrow one like in all the semis. And down the landing, open the bathroom door, the light's on. At first, for perhaps a second, I don't notice anything. You know, looking at my fly, looking at the loo. I've already got it out, I'm bursting, when I see that I'm peeing onto *hair*. I look up and, my God, it's so difficult.

He's rubbing and rubbing his thighs again, moving to and

fro and sucking his lower lip in and out.

— I just look down and carry on peeing. I'm so scared, so scared, that I … I don't do anything. Don't scream, don't run to her. I just finish and walk out. I think my eyes were open but I couldn't see anything.

— Next thing that I remember is calling Aatjie. I'm downstairs in the lounge. 'Aatjie, come here. Aatjie.' In a sort of loud whisper. My voice sounded funny, like someone else's with a little squeak in it. The others became quiet. Aatjie comes through from the kitchen with his cup. We stand and look at each other, my hands are shaking like scared mice. I take his hand and pull him, without speaking, gesturing with my head, and so I lead him up to the bathroom. I stop him outside the door, stand facing him with my arms like this, preventing him from getting in. 'Aatjie, it's Jess. She's in there. There's something wrong, Aatjie, I think, I, think she's … dead.' And as I say the word I lean forward and hold him, put my head onto his shoulder. He holds me for about so long, then pushes me away, past me and into the room. She's lying in the bath, and her head is shaved. Her head is shaved! And there's blood, the bath is all red, all red with blood. Her head, her shoulders, her breasts with brown nipples, her knees and her hands are showing above the blood. Her hands, her fingers with red in the cracks between. Glenda, I can't I can't …

Billy's rocking, twisting his neck, his breath is shaking.

— I did nothing, nothing. It was Aatjie that went to her, that shook her smooth head, calling her name. 'Jess, Jessica!' slapping on her cheek. He tries to lift her body out of the bloody water, the water that's getting cold now. 'Come and help me man Billy, don't jus stand there.'

— And I go and take her legs, under the knees, putting my hands in her blood, wetting my sleeves. 'No, get a towel. Put it on the floor. There.' I drop the legs again, they slide, still warm, into the water. I fetch a towel and lay it on the floor. In among the hair, there's hair everywhere. The tiles are slidy underfoot from the hair. Then I go and take her legs again, hands into the bloody water. We put her down on the towel. Aatjie says, 'It's her wrists, go get a sheet to tear up. Move, she's still bleeding.' And I run for Arn's bedroom, pull a sheet from the bed, back to the bathroom. The sheet won't tear. I tug at it with my teeth. Aatjie nudges me on the arm with the scissors. He's found them on the floor. You know, she must have used those scissors to cut her hair with. Her hair! I kept finding bits of it, for days, weeks afterwards. I'd find it in the pantry, or on the furniture, or look at my jersey, and there'd be a piece of that long reddish hair.

Aatjie had tried for quarter of an hour to resuscitate her. Breathed into her mouth, turned her head to let the air out, pushing on the chest. Fuad, whose religion forbade him even so much as to touch a woman, much less a *Chris* woman. A dying infidel. He'd carried on while the strips of sheet got red, and then stopped getting redder. Billy had told the others — *How not to tell Vaughn, still full of acid, coming down, oh God, oh God, oh God* — Told Arn first.

— Arn, come here. No, Vaughn, I'll talk to you later — whispering — Listen, it's Jessica, she's cut her wrists, upstairs in the bath, Aatjie's doing mouth to mouth, what about Vaughn?

— Has anyone phoned an ambulance? No.

Arn runs, boom boom boom three steps, upstairs to the phone on the landing. Billy hears him dialling, cursing, rattling the receiver, dialling and starting to talk. Cheryl comes through, sees Billy's face, bloodless white.

— William. What is it? What's going on?

Meanwhile, in the kitchen, Vaughn is feeling his mind, a great unending lake, being sucked into a Victoria Falls of paranoia. *This is the sea at world's end.* Arnold's voice cuts through it all, through the house, through Billy guppying at Cheryl, through Cheryl's worried expression, her concern, through the waterfall of Vaughn's mind.

— She's dying! She's *dying*! May be dead already — into the phone. And everyone's crowding into the bathroom, pressing over Aatjie struggling to make her breathe. — Breathe, breathe damn it — and thumping her chest — I've phoned, they're coming — and — Strong, we must be strong — from Vaughn who is standing upright, puffing his chest, clenching his fists. The departing acid has tossed him this last gift: *Run the bravery programs, the soldier's programs. Go rigid.*

Billy walks out to look for a letter, a note, and finds himself standing in her room picking up and putting down her things. Cosmetics, an old cut-crystal atomiser. On the bed, propped neatly in the middle between the plumped-out cushions sits Eddy, her ancient darned threadbare Teddy bear and next to the bed the book she'd been reading: Roy Campbell's translations of Saint John.

And I flew up so high, so high

That in the end I met my quarry.

There's her sewing-machine on the dressing-table, a new Bernina. *A neat heap of unmarked exam papers. The other staff'll curse her for that. No, nothing.* It's all in order, though, lifting the counterpane, he can see that crumpled clothes and shoes have been shoved in under the bed.

— Anyway, she died. Aatjie couldn't save her. When the ambulance people got there they told us. They were really heavy. Really judgmental. You know, a death in the vice den. Her mother came, it was all in the press. The one who seemed to take it best was Vaughn, and he'd been tripping. On LSD. I expected him to dive into the world's all-time bummer, but he seemed to bounce back. I don't know … we lost contact a few weeks after that. And Cheryl was really nice to me. Like a mother. After it was all over, as the first light was coming in, when there was nothing we could do, she and I made love, and I felt really guilty making love after that, I mean guilty that I enjoyed it, that I forgot for a time. And she, uh, she ... she had an orgasm and she cried while she was coming, and I'll never know if it was from joy or because of Jess, or both. I told you she used to cry a lot.

— That was really when I stopped being a hippy. Just got right out of it. Cheryl and I were married, what, about three or four months later, in Durban. You know the rest of it, all the Cheryl stuff. Well, most of it, the big bits.

A Coherent Philosophy

22 June 1986

The briefing had been business-like and factual, but had taken longer than he'd expected. There's one of those silly laws about it: It always takes longer and costs more.

— These are the procedures to call. These partitions are for your use. The operating system allows the following ...

Usual stuff.

— Here's your security card. It expires the day you're finished here. Your passwords will be, please memorise this: for sign-on, 3342 followed by ALPHA SINGEL. Upper or lower case. You can set up your own partition access codes, and make sure that's the first thing you do. This folder contains the specifications for MacFarlaine's version, as well as the previous two systems. Just skim through them to make sure you're not using the same method. The guys in Security know you'll be here. They'll look after you. Here's the coffee machine, programmer's best friend. This is your terminal.

An empty room, blue-fibre carpet, cream plastic-topped desk. The terminal isn't IBM, but if you put the three magic letters there on the left, the difference would vanish. There's a calendar on the wall with sepia line-drawings of Cape Scenes. One unopenable sheet of grey glass looks out onto the service courtyard. Sewage drains, pipes. He can make out a bottle of antiseptic, standing on the shelf behind a frosted-glass window across there.

— I'll need access to a tape drive. I'm bringing a few

special routines up, stuff that'll be useful to me.

— I'll tell Sakkie. When you bring the tape, give it to him. He's the head of night-time operations, down in the computer room. Little fellow with a grey moustache. You can communicate with him on the intercom here. Four seven, got that?

— Four seven. Sakkie. For the tape. No problem.

— The doors. Van der Poel downstairs will let you in. You use the card like this, oh, you've got them at your work. Each door has a card-reader on it. Yours, for instance, will only let you get as far as here. Are there any problems?

— No, no problems.

— Hello, you awake?

There are sounds from the bedroom: Sue's flat in Mowbray. She's in there reading and almost asleep. For the last week it'd been nothing but poetry, looting Billy's bookshelf, her own, finding in Clarke's a hardly-read copy of a translation of Hikmet! *When the eyes stay open and you carry on reading but the words, the printed words are already a dream. Rose, my rose.*

— Hello little pig. I'm in here reading.

— Oink. Who's the pig in there under the warm duvet?

— Me. Your eyes are red again. One day those screens will blind you, you'll have to get great thick specs to peer at your programs or whatever it is that you look at.

He leans over to kiss her and her face feels warm from being half asleep. Her breath is sweet like it always is. A bit like cow's breath sweet. *How does she do it, mine's like an ashtray, yuk, she must love me!*

— I'm tired. I've got a sore back. Bad posture. What time's it?

— Quarter past ten. There's half a pie in the kitchen but it must be cold by now. Won't you make some hot milk?

— Okay.

— Why were you so long? You said that you'd be back before nine.

— I told you not to wait up or anything. I was being briefed for that moonlighting job. It's almost worth a holiday in Botswana, think of that. They're a bunch of assholes, worried about kiddie hackers sneaking in and stealing their precious data. Had to show me everything — his voice going up half an octave — even how to work the coffee machine. It just took longer, that's all.

— All right, all right. I was only asking.

— And I was only telling you. Hot milk. With Milo or honey, Honey?

They lie in bed together. She can feel him warm against her back, his few chest-hairs tickly. Can feel his breathing and, yes, his heartbeat dimly there. His breath comes slowly and warm past her ear. One knee nuzzling into the back of hers, he shifts. His penis is floppy, pressed against her buttocks.

Her one hand is curled up to her shoulder, the other is down in the warmth of her groin; between the finger and thumb is a curl of pubic hair: baby blanket, comfort. A soft unconscious smoothing of the little ringlet, wrapping it round and round, rubbing.

— Sue.

— Yes.

— What's the worst thing that ever happened to you? Really the worst.

— I don't know lovey. Maybe it's you?

— No, jokes aside. The worst.

— Well, it depends on what you mean by worst, doesn't it? It could be sorest. That would be the time I broke my collarbone. Or most embarassing. Ermm, I'm not telling that one.

— No, I mean the *worst* thing. If you were given a special sort of eraser and could go back into your life and

wipe out just one thing, what would it be? The thing that's
happened to you, that you hate most.

— You're raving again. Your 'worst' could be anything.
The thing which *I* think worst. Or the thing that, if I could
change it then, would help me most now. Something that I
hated while it was happening? I mean, take marrying
Alvin. I was so happy. I'd psyched myself up, been psyched up by mom and, well, the family, for months. To be
happy. The bride's day, when the man is only her groom.
If I could undo that, who would I be now?

He doesn't answer. After a while, he says:

— I can't sleep. I'm going home. I might try to write
something.

— Can I come with you? I won't get in the way, I'll just
go to sleep in your bed.

In the car she has the hot-water bottle on her lap.

— Billy, do you have a coherent philosophy? I mean, a
way of understanding and acting in the world?

— Uh, no. I've had them from time to time, though.
You know what a backslider I am.

— But your woman, Mylia, she has. She knows where
she's going.

— Implying that I don't. Know where I'm going. Right
now I'm going home.

— No. On the contrary. Implying that you do. And that
she somehow is it. But you still won't take responsibility
for her.

— Well, all right. But you're talking about the borders
of going crazy. The borders of split personalities.

— Rubbish. From what I've read, from what you've told
me, she's absolutely sane. More so than you. Do you
know what that means? I don't think you've even thought
about it, what it means.

— I think about it most of the time. When I'm not
thinking about you and work and things, that is.

— But, ummh. Somewhere in you there's a sane calm being. With a coherent philosophy, with a way of under-standing things, and you've given her a face, a form. You can *talk* to her. But she's also *you*. You're very lucky. Most of us have to grope around in the dark to find her, if we even believe she's there.

— Let's go to Maggie's and have an Irish.

— Now? It's nearly twelve.

— They're open all night. But we can go home if you want to catch up on your sleep.

— Home. Please.

'Mylia, do you have a coherent philosophy?'

'I don't follow you. What is a "coherent philosophy"?'

'Well, a way of understanding the world, of how you fit into it, a way that guides your actions.'

'We have struggled against such a thing for nearly two hundred years. But we're always failing. Yes, I think you could say that I have a particular set of ways. Of being, of doing things and so on. Like paths over a hill. Little roads that we walk on, when all the hill stands under the sky. The next thing you're going to be asking me to recite the details of all this, aren't you?'

'Am I bothering you?'

'No. What could be richer than an exchange with another world?'

She came forward and held my hand again, in that ges-ture of hers. Her eyes, her golden eyes!

'Imagine a plain, a big open plain. On the one side is ice and snow, and on the other is heat, burnt desert. Some-where in the middle runs a road. In the middle it's pleasant, with the normal variation of the days and nights, of the moons and the seasons. Down this runs a path. The one side, let's say the hot, is all rage and oppression, the other is abjection, submission, slavery. No, a plain's not a good image.'

'*I can picture it clearly*'

'*That's the trouble. You're probably filling it up with streams and flowers. The image is getting too much of its own life to hold my meaning.*

'*Let's call it a spectrum. From oppression to slavery. The one causing the other, endlessly. Somewhere in the middle is a slender and blurring region called equality. Think of it as a road for us to walk on, in our relation to one another, to all the exchanges of life and the intermatrices. That is really the sum of my coherent philosophy. When we tip one way or the other, everything goes awry. The rest is only the ramblings of an old woman.*' *She massages the palm of my hand, the ball of my thumb, with strong fingers and smiles broadly.*

He turns the machine off, watches the screen's afterglow in the dark study. Goes through to the bedroom, undresses, lies up against her till he stops shivering. The starting point of his dream is of using the Crencor magnetic card to open the briefcase.

Hummous and Dried Blood

26 June 1986

The chickpeas and the sesame and cumin seeds come from
Atlas, up in the Malay Quarter, *Die Bo-Kaap*, spice and
incense smell still lingering about them. Cucumbers are
from the vegetable man with his old blue Chev bakkie; he
comes every Saturday. Red tomatoes sit plump on the cut-
ting-board.

*Chickpeas're nearly ready now, taste one, mmm, still a bit
hard. Dough, that's ready. Move the tomatoes, flour the
board, spoon the dough all stringy with a yeast smell onto the
board, roll it into a ball. Flour, a bit more, the dough's soft
and firm and rubbery and makes little popping sounds as
yeast-bubbles are squeezed out. Knead, making a bull's head.
A face, anyone's face and hit it.*

— Hey, c'mere. Who would you like to hit? A good
whack in the face?

— I don't know. Maybe Alvin.

He models a face, Alvin. *Hmm, big nose with a bump.
Two fingers in for eyes. No, it's too round. Squeeze it out a
bit and hold it up for her to hit.*

— There we are. Take a smack.

She pounds the dough one-two-three. Her face screws
up for a final shot. Alvin.

— Bastard! ... he *was a* real bastard.

— Is.

— I want to make one for you to clobber.

— All right. While we're doing Exes, let's do Cheryl.

And Laura, I want to take a shot at Laura!

Her turn to make the face. *Cheryl ... this is tricky ground.* But the dough is too spongy to model well anyway. What emerges looks like a cartoon of a gawping old woman. *Good.* A dishcloth gets draped over for hair. He's excited, giggling, doing that foot-bouncing boxer's dance, commentating:

— Bam-bam. Bam. And one with the left! And a hook bambam. Now Laura.

Laura's more difficult, more recent, less than eighteen months. Laura's the big one, the shadow that Sue feels hanging, critical, over her. With her diamond jewellery and her rich parents. *Pull out a piece for the nose, poke in thumbs. The cloth again.*

— There we go.

— And he's got her in the corner against the ropes. He's giving it to her really good. Bam, one two.

The chickpeas boil over, hissing onto the stoveplate. Take the lid off, they're done, turn it off. Knead the dough into a long roll, take a knife, cut into two, four, eight. Make eight little balls, flour them.

The oven on, let it get up to 'Massima', the crooked needle's still at 'Media'. An Italian stove, the sign says Zoppas. *Who's ever heard of a Zoppas stove? But the big Z has been designed fancy to look almost like an OM.* Om, oppas. *Papas, Medea.*

She takes two onions and halves them vertically, lays them flat-side-down on the board. Ends off, skins off and into the enamel basin for the trash.

— Wait, that's the blunt knife. Use this one, it's sharper.

She cuts them into half-rings *with this, yes, much better knife. Crunch crunch crunch.* Her eyes go weepy. Now the other way, crunch. Scrape the little squares into the blue bowl, *look, it's a Castles of England.*

— Where did you get this?

— Junk shop. Why?

— Our family used to have a complete Castles of England service. I must have eaten off this pattern thousands of times. Reminds me of my mum. Funny I haven't noticed it before.

— I hauled it out from down there for the first time in ages.

Now the tomatoes. *Ah, the kettle's ready*. Wipe eyes. Empty the enamel basin into the bin. Fill it with big steamy water and slide them in easy so they don't splash. And he's kneading the dough balls into bread-plate-sized circles, so thick. The first two are waiting on the oven tray. The heat's up now and in they go.

The tomatoes. Their skins have split tight in the hot water, bleeding those little red particles. Peel and dice them, wet and swampy in your hand, drop the bits in with the onions. Fresh sweet basil from the garden, salt, oil. Mix it up and set it aside.

Billy opens the oven and floods the room with the scent of hot pitta bread.

— The bloody first ones never pop open properly.

— That's all right. We'll put them underneath. When are you going to start on the hummous? They'll be here in just on an hour.

— They'll be late. I'm starting now. Watch.

Watch him peel the garlic, four big cloves. They go in the blender first. Next olive oil, cumin seeds, salt.

— Shit, the sesame seeds. Turn that plate on will you? Ja.

And the cast-iron pan, the small one, is filled with the little seeds poured from a brown-paper packet, like grass seeds. *Open Sesame, and all of Ali Baba's treasures roll at your feet. Groaning with gems*. First the spice-shop's smell exudes from the seeds and it's followed by rich nutty roasting as they swell and pop in the pan.

— I must love you.

— Why?

— Because you're the first person I've ever shown any-
thing I've written. I used to squirrel everything away. Even
Cheryl and Laura didn't get to see anything. Especially
Laura. Do you realise what a rare privilege that is?

— No, your highness — curtseying — but I take your
lordship's word for it. Her ladyship commands me to tell
you that she must love you too.

Load the sesame seeds still hot into the coffee-grinder.
Try not to spill, they jump like fleas. Close it, hold the lid
down because the bloody little closing mechanism's
broken, grind. Electric Zizzzzz. They turn to paste, a thick
ochre golden peanutbuttery paste. A tongue-contracting
pleasure of roasted smell rushes from it as you open.
Spoon it out into the blender jug, over the oil and garlic.
Put the coffee-grinder away, replace the blender on its
motor.

— Why? Must she love me?

— Why, your Highness, it's either you've got her
enslaved, or it's that she loves you. In all deference to
your highness, why else would she put up with all your
crap?

For the lemon juice, slice a lemon — Pass the knife. Ta
— onto the squeezer, ripe sour juice. Pour some in, keep
the rest aside. Lemon rinds into the bin. Now the chickpeas, like little boiled chickens, plump. Pour them into the
blender steam hot, with their water.

— Garbanzos, always thought that name was onomato-
poeia.

— Is that how you pronounce it? I used to avoid saying
the word in English tuts. But I haven't heard them going
garbanzogarbanzo.

— No. It's because of the way you fart afterwards.
GaaaaarBANZO! Oo, the oven. Do the breads will you.

Put the lid on the blender now, switch it on. The chickpeas disintegrate and go all thick and porridgy. Stir — No,

no. Not with my best spoon, pass me that one. Thanks —
Keep stirring while it grinds, missing the ravening little
blades. Taste, *a bit more salt*.

*Humus is something you dig into the ground. This is
hummous! With the* h *pronounced* ch *as in loch*. Dish it
into the big green bowl from the potters' fair scraping the
last bits out with the long double-thick-malted spoon.

— He who sups with the devil hath need of a long
spoon.

— But she who sups with him just watches him use it.

He smooths the hummous down, cuts a trellis pattern of
grooves in it. First the rest of the lemon juice, then
sprinkle paprika over the top. Lots of it.

— Look, dried blood.

— Ooer, you'll turn me into a vegetarian.

— Maybe the food'll turn you into one. You know that
all of this is for Arnold. Won't defile himself with the
merest smell of blood, but I swear he was wearing a pig-
skin jacket.

Now more olive oil, sprinkled spirally on top. Add a few
chopped chives.

— Hey, look at the time. You do the table and I'll make
the cucumber stuff.

— *I'll* make the cucumber stuff. You are quite the
kitchen Madam tonight though. You can *do the table*. I
was waiting for you to offer to lay it, and then I was going
to say, 'Your sex-drive will be the death of me.'

— Ooh, touchy. Touchy touchy feely. Isn't that from
Pieter-Dirk Uys? Wonder where he ripped it off?

— From me. Oh, and won't you open the red now.

— Shit, there's the doorbell. I'll get it. I don't believe it,
they're bloody well early. Well, they'll just have to hover
around while we finish up here.

Colleen and Arnold stand smiling in the doorway. She's
carrying the bottle of wine and flowers. Big shouts of jubi-

lation, the men hug. Billy turns to Colleen for one of her half-wet kisses.

— Flowers! For me! Colleen you guilty girl, you've been seeing someone else behind my back. This schmuck. Arn, skin me brother.

He holds his hand out, slap it as hard as you can.

— Now your turn. Smack! All right!

— How're you doing, Billy me boy? You're looking well.

— I feel tired. Work. But I'm well and happy. Yes. I'm in love, oh shit this is Sue; Sue, Arn and Colleen. I was saying I'm happy and I've been writing again. Every spare moment bashing away at the word processor up in the study. I love it. And hate it sometimes. And you two? Where's Brucie? I told you to bring him and put him to sleep on my bed. Sue was dying to meet him.

— He'd have your mattress soaking wet in twenty minutes. Mom's looking after him. Actually it's very convenient, and she dotes on the little bugger.

Wine is opened, ordinary Tassies. The places get set on the table, on the big blue-gingham tablecloth, with half the flowers quietly glowing calendula yellow in the middle. Flowers; Billy looks at them, lovely, lovely, but what's this? The flowers shine against the blue cloth and he sees Mylia's lines of fire burning through them, through the wooden chairs, the floor; the fine blaze of life, without warning. *Look away, fetch the food in.*

How long does a South African conversation take to turn to politics? Now, in the State of Emergency, now when everything seems so desperate? Ten minutes, twenty? Half an hour if you're good friends, or if you're meeting for the first time and have to get over the hump of — What do you do? Oh, sales? Is that interesting? — the bottleneck of working out class and kind.... Colleen has this idea ...

— I want to print some letters, oh a hundred or so. And each one'll say:

> Dear Sir/Madam,
>   In these times I would like to remind you that decisions of state have real human consequences. Our society is made entirely of ordinary persons like you and me, with hearts and minds and hopes and dreams. Please accept this sample of real human blood as a token of the suffering in our land, and bear it in mind when taking decisions which may affect others.

— And there'd be a drop of my blood in a neat square on the paper. I'd have to cut my finger for that, but it could be worth it. And I'll send them to everyone, marked Private and Confidential. To P.W. and to all the cabinet and to, well, to the ANC in Lusaka, how would I get their address?

— Will you sign it? With your own name?

— Of course. Colleen Mary Theresa Clark. Number four, Balmyra Mansions, Protea Crescent, Vredehoek. Eight thousand and one.

Arn looks proprietorial and perhaps a little uncomfortable, says nothing.

— We could make it into a chain letter! Send it to friends as well, get them to send it on — Sue's idea, and the two of them go into a huddle in the kitchen, over the steaming stove.

The food is brought in, the candles lit.

— Arnold, remember how you used to make us say grace? Say one for us now.

Sue's embarrassed. Colleen sighs and rolls her eyes. But Arnold, though it be only a hobby now, is still the Mystic Prince.

— All right. I know, there's an old Dissenters' grace. Well, I think it's a grace. It goes like this, can we hold hands?

This is what the scarecrow said
From the field where he lay:
'My face is made of an old goat's skin,
And my hair is yellow hay.

But my form is the human form,
And the human is Divine.'
God's blessings on this food, kind folk
And on all thee and thine.

— Amen. This is our body, folks. Let's eat.

The Food Moment arrives: everyone is quiet, looking. There are pitta breads in the basket, salads, fiery green-chilli pickles. Split the flat bread open and stuff it with the hummous and the tomato salad and the tsatsiki and just a dab of the chilli. Eat with the sour red wine. The lines of fire run through the food.

Arnold and Billy, as always, talk about the past, about old friends and *those* days, the camaraderie of a self-defined élite. Sue makes Greek coffee, muddy and bitter.

Afterwards she takes Colleen off to show her around. Billy steers the conversation back into the present. But really a sort of hypothetical present, something he wants help in thinking about:

— Arn, if you were, let's say, the, well, the Branch. Or something like that, state security. And you wanted to get your hands on a computer. Not a dinky little PC or whatever but big kit. You know, a really kosher mainframe, something that could handle all the database requirements. What would you do?

— I'd toddle out to the nearest mainframe store and buy one. They're not short of coins or something. What do you think their annual budget for computing runs to? Fifty, a hundred million?

— Easily. More. But you can't just toddle out to buy one. Remember the Sullivan Code? Even those big mainframe bastards aren't supplying their stuff for that sort of use any more. Or pretending they're not. A little moral schmoral looks really natty on the annual report.

— Well then I'd set up a front, or get someone else to. — He makes the finger-rubbing gesture of lubrication. — Shouldn't be a problem. Buy it and just move it on.

— But that kind of deal's not a one-off. You know, it's an ongoing affair. Maintenance, upgrades, new software ...

— So make the front ongoing, set up a whole fake company. Is that what you're planning to do? I'll come in with you for, say, twenty per cent. — He puts on his Evil Scheming Capitalist look.

— Nah, fuck off. You couldn't run a hundred yards, much less a front for the Branch.

They hear the sound of the printer going upstairs and the women come down with a sheet of paper: the letter, a first sample. Colleen places it on the rug in the middle of the sitting-room. Conversation stops while they watch. Sue hands her a needle. She holds it like a pen or a dart, aimed at her left index finger. Pauses, stabs in deeper than necessary and the first drop of blood oozes out. She holds it up for everyone to see, the drop slowly growing there on the whorls. Over the paper where they've ruled the little square. Drop.

Encrypted, of Course
27–29 June 1986

— Raj, if you had to screw up a system, I mean a whole mainframe system, how would you go about it?

— I'd give you the specs, let you write it all by yourself. It couldn't be any worse than some systems I've seen screwed up, though.

— Verreee funneee. But that's not what I mean. It's just a hypothetical question.

— Well, that would depend on if you were writing it from scratch or if there was already a good system in there. New stuff's easy to screw up. As you of all people should know. But if you wanted to wipe out something that's already there, you'd have to get the backups. Your move. And you'd have to write interrupts which pre-empted whatever security and logging procedures are installed. In a hierarchy.

— You and your bloody little knights.

Sue looks up at him hovering over her with an expectant air.

— You keep on giving me these fragments. I want more, I want the whole thing. Come on, more, more.

She makes little beckoning gestures with all her fingers. Gimme.

— You can't have more, because there isn't more.

— I mean her. It's her I want to know about. What she thinks, what she does. The whole structure of her views and her person.

— Hell, give me a chance. I only write it as it comes. It's supposed to be a story, you know, not Wittgenstein or Engels or something. You've really fixated on the woman, haven't you? There are others there, you know. What about the contemplation master, Eenirh? Don't you want to know about him?

— Ja, I suppose so. How many pages are there now?

— About a hundred and fifty or so. That'll probably boil down to less than a hundred after I've sifted through.

— Listen, I'll tell you what. Let's go over everything you've got and extract a, well, a portrait of her and the way her life and her ideology hang together. I'll write it up for you, you know, organise it properly. For your appendix. Have you still got that profile, the two-page one that you showed me?

— Aren't you interested in the other stuff? In the scene, the *human drama*, in the ecology, God I've worked out a whole ecology.

— Of course. But I'm mostly interested in who she is. I want to feel her as a whole human. What she does and thinks is only interesting if it comes alive in her. And in you. And I'm not actually all that interested in the Utopian stuff.

— Crap. It's not a Utopia. A Utopia's a very specialised sort of thing. It's a — it's just a fucking Science Fiction novel. Which I happen to be enjoying writing.

— I'd only read one in my whole life before I met you. *The Day of the Triffids*, by John Wyndham. And I don't think I even finished it. I don't understand why it has to be Science Fiction anyway. It's so out there, so unconnected.

— Well, how can I say, I can't have her here. I mean, I can't explore these ideas on Earth, now. There's no place where you could locate this kind of stuff. And I'm not writing a tract. Where I could sort of, you know, just hold forth. I want to let it all *live*. Imagine it in practice.

— You're such a fuckwit, you know. Listen to you. Why

not *put* it into practice?

— I am. I'm writing a novel. And I don't need you falling over your own tongue contradicting yourself only to undermine me like that. Just in case you didn't realise it, Science Fiction, fantasy, is the root of all the other literatures. Only a pity about the science part of it; but they're all unreal, unless it's documentary. All imagined, and all fiction. Right from what, Homer? I think fantasy is the realm of the unconscious, of new discoveries. It's very important.

— My God, the arrogance of it. You can't hear me, you try not to hear me; and you always cover everything up in a garbage of talk talk talk. Why not just try following something through to where it comes from? I think you're writing Mylia to avoid being her. Then you may have to actually change yourself, and that would mean changing the world too. Isn't that what she does? I couldn't care a stuff about all your grandiose ideas on fiction and so on. But what I can feel is a quality of sanity in you, a quality that's trying to come out in the book.

— Just leave it, okay? Just leave it.

— Sue.

— Mm-mm?

He's come down with a handful of pages. It's new copy without all the little margin notes, deletions, pencil scribblings. (Yes, even with the word-processor.)

— There's something funny with that Crencor bunch. I'm slowly starting to get the idea that they're not what they say they are. They've got all that kit just sitting there and all they seem to do is *guard* it. There's no midnight run, no big update, ageing of the policies, whatever. They don't seem to do any *business*. And everything's done on remote. I discovered today that there are only two terminals in the building. And I'm using one of them. The rest go out to God knows where.

— Isn't all this supposed to be very hush-hush?

— Ja. Very. But *you're* hardly going to rush off and expose them.

— I might well. What would it be worth?

— I'll boil you in midnight oil.

— What've you got there? More? Come and sit here. Finish my horrid sherry for me. Let's see.

— Only two new bits. It's still very unworked. Have a look. It's the part where the troops come. This is the hard part, and I don't really know how to handle it. How they'll handle it. Remember, they've captured one of the weapons people. That is, the state, the army have. This other's one of her little lectures. It goes on the front of the chapter where he works in the cloth-printing shop.

Troops have arrived. They came by what look like hovercraft, moving in up the valley from the south-west. Four big craft, carrying about eighty men. They stopped in the central square, and the roaring echo of their engines slowly died.

Armoured soldiers filed out, carrying energy weapons. They surrounded the vehicles and stood facing outwards with the guns held across their chests, sticking up at an angle. Hurried efficient movement, obviously much drilled.

I ran out onto the library steps, and stood in the shadow of the doorway watching. The dust thinned out, the air stood still. The soldiers remained locked in their formation. Nobody from the village paid any attention and the three people who had been in the square got up and left, walking slowly and casually.

Half an hour passed, with the big vehicles just sitting there, surrounded by immobile men. I noticed the deliberation with which the librarian and the two others in the building ignored them. It seemed planned, as if this was the agreed thing to do. No-one had told me, warned me. I felt frightened, menaced by the grim potential of the craft in the square.

A man, obviously an officer, came towards us, sur-

rounded by a phalanx of the armoured troops. The library is certainly the biggest building facing onto the square, and they must have mistaken it for an administrative centre or temple. I hid myself behind a cupboard and watched. Having had a lot of trouble getting permission to enter this region, I had no intention of calling my presence here into question.

First the officer's guards came, over the dusty paving. Two of them jogging in front, two more accompanying him, walking. The last two walked backwards with weapons held up, the eye slits in their helmets moving, scanning the trees, the buildings. The officer was tall and dark. He had his helmet off so that I could see his face. It reminded me of Mylia's, but perhaps this is because both are foreign to me in similar ways.

The librarian was at her desk, a young woman, perhaps twenty. She looked up and smiled as they came in.

'Can I help you? You're looking for a book or a crystal?'

'Tell me where I can find the village Headman. And please be co-operative. We aren't trying to make trouble.'

'My name is Yemia. I will be pleased to help you with any queries concerning the library.' She was doing well, her smile and air of friendliness holding up.

'I am the Armage Kinten, of the Eleventh Wing of the Tannur surface force. I want you to take me to the village Headman. There's no need to be afraid of us.' His tone even and polite.

'We have no Headman here, Kinten. You may talk to me if you wish.'

'I don't need to waste time with a librarian. Who is in charge of the village?'

'The Mother leads us.'

'And where is she?'

She smiled again. 'You'll find her in the fields or up on

*the hill. She seldom comes here, into the library. Rather
the library goes out to her.'*

'Her name, what's her name?'

*'We don't call her by any particular name. Sometimes
Matrix.' (The word can also mean sweet-breasted and is a
common name for women of the Matrifax.)*

'Describe her.'

*'Why, she looks like me.' She passed her hands in front
of her body. 'But older, much older.'*

*I thought at first that she might be describing Mylia. I
must have turned her into a leader of sorts, in my mind.*

*'You will get a message to her. Tell her that I want to
speak to her here in the square. At sunset. I shall wait
under that tree.' He turned and left, his men trotting
ahead of him.*

— See, I stopped there. Before anything actually happens.

— But quite a lot has happened. They've got a particular style. The style has happened.

— Ja, I know. When I sat down to write that, all I knew
was that the troops had arrived, that the village would
have to deal with it. And I've got a name for the place.
Imbrast. It's in the dictionary too. But I pronounce it
Imbr-ast.

— I don't like it. It sounds silly.

— Do you like Johannesburg? Or Pofadder?

— I'm not sure about all this Mother business either.
You must clear that up a bit, otherwise it'll just go all
mushy, into a sort of new-age Mother Nature puddle.
Make it more clear somewhere that she's not a woman,
not even female.

— I thought that was clear, it's supposed to be. I'll tell
you what, I'll have an appendix that explains it. The
Mother.

— How's yours?

— What? Oh my mom. All right, I suppose. I thought

you meant my appendix. Her letters are all the same. The
garden and the cats and what Eva Kaplan has to say about
the neighbours. I hate old age. Why?

— Just wondered. Pass the other bit. Ta.

— It's just a fragment, really. Hardly a page.

*Mylia was playing a hand-clapping game with two chil-
dren. Seeing me, they got a serious look and ran off towards the big square.*

'*Are you their teacher, too?*'

'*There are no reserved roles here, Peter. Everyone can
be anything, and if we do things, we do them together. We
study together. If an adult learns something together with
a child, that's an excellent thing. But is it really teaching?
And if the adult knows it already, there is the delight of
learning it again.*

'*What about things that just simply have to be learned?*'

'*Of course there are certain things that must be learned
by rote. Multiplication tables, writing. But there are no
teachers specifically for those things. Everyone in the community, everyone teaches the children the rote things, especially the older people. We take turns, there's supposed
to be a roster but we don't really use it any more. The
children have taken charge of that and they make sure that
they get us all to come down to their place to play and
teach. Everywhere else in Imbr-ast, children may come to
learn things, by working and watching work, by talking
and listening. Knowledge is to share, especially with the
small ones.*'

'*And you were teaching those kids a hand-clapping
game?*'

'*I was playing with them. We already knew the game. In
fact, I learned it from them. Tell me a story, Peter. A
story that your people tell.*'

The sudden shift takes me by surprise. A story.

'*The version of this story that I read was written about
two hundred and fifty years ago. The story itself is much*

older. It comes from a small island in the north of our planet. Some of my ancestors may have come from there. The version I read was in verse, but I can't remember the form of it, just the story.'

And I tell her the story of Oisin, the old Irish warlord, leader of the Fienna, and Niamh, the fairy who took him for three hundred years to the land across the sea. She listens carefully, ignoring my apologies when I forget bits.

'... but when he bent from his horse to help them move the stone — I told you what a horse is?'

'Yes.'

'Well, the saddle strap broke, and he fell to the ground.'

And so on until it gets dark. By the time I've finished, there are three listeners, Mylia and two dark men who hear out my words in solemn silence.

The file structures are all in these reserved libraries. Load Raj's magic collection of assembler routines into a partition of their own. Now let's have a look at what these bastards are up to. Interesting if nothing else. Hmm, first to disable the logging procedure, make a fake log.

Raj's lovely little program sort of, well, moves in and nobbles the logging stuff, they should hardwire it. Just sits there really and interrupts the file usage calls. And writes innocent-looking ones from this file that I've set up. Dave's stuff a piece of old toffee, he once showed me on paper how it works.

— You write the passwords back into the program sector, like this: the program actually writes its own source, with the passwords set in as a sort of Data Statement here. It's the first thing you do, and there's no little file anywhere with the dangeroos lurking in it. Encrypted, of course.

— So the program's a hell of a lot bigger than it needs to be.

— No, not actually. It needs to write itself, so there's no redundancy as such.

The black keys click under his fingers. A hundred and twenty words a minute.

Wonder if that was a breach of the Crencor fine print? He didn't tell me what it was for, just the theory. Bet they could get you for theory....

Okay, disassemble it command by command and dump the results on the printer here. Oho, here's the little encryption routine, lovely, Dave. Lift the routine out. Into another file, here. And here are the scrambled passwords themselves. Cunning, really, they're manipulated at very low level. Now if we can just see what the routine does, yes generate a random number here, store it over there.... Ah.

And the whole thing falls apart in his hands like a wooden Chinese puzzle, with Raj's little intercept ticking away. Well, silent actually. The files open like petals of a flower, and the system is waiting for him. The half-finished coffee gets cold, skins over.

An Individual

1 July 1986

Towards nightfall the village gathered, coming in slowly from the fields, the workshops, the kitchens. Children came, old men and women, people whom I'd never seen. Sick people were brought from their rooms on stretchers. There was no deliberate movement towards the square; rather a slow drifting, a kind of diffusion, casual and careful.

By the time the sun went down everyone was there, forming a horseshoe around the soldiers in the middle. People under the trees, quietly talking, eating, and, yes, laughing. I tried to count them, to estimate the numbers. Somewhere between a thousand and fifteen hundred. Floodlights from the heavy grey combat cars cast long shadows.

The troops remained motionless around their vehicles, holding their weapons against their chests, their mirror-finish armour caught and distorted the end of the sunset. A helmet gleamed. The door in the foremost car opened and Kinten emerged, followed by his guard. He was carrying what must have been a microphone. He looked around at the people, went back and said something into the doorway.

Two more soldiers came out, bringing a young woman. She was as tall as the bigger of them, with dark hair in three plaits, wearing a blue coverall and wrapped in a pale shawl. Sitting on the library steps, near Mylia, I was too far away to make out her face against the lights in the dusklight. They pushed her forward to stand next to the Armage. There was a murmur, a whoosh of breath, and the assembled people slowly fell silent. A baby's high crying came from behind the trees.

The Armage spoke into the instrument in his hand and the voice came from everywhere. From the floor, the air, from out of the library, from the parked vehicles, the darkening sky.

'We wish to speak to your leader, the one called Matrix.'

People shuffled, remained silent. A shout from the back of the crowd: 'She is with us now.' Another voice: 'Why?'

'This woman Nahir Rurik', he gestured at his captive, 'was involved in the sabotage of the South-Western Ocean Harvesting Project six days ago. She was captured by men of the Seventeenth Wing and has been identified as coming from Imbr-ast. We have evidence that there were at least five others with her, and there is good reason to believe that at least some of these are being harboured here. I want to talk to your leader, this Matrix. Will you please step forward.'

To my right, a man started to sing, sure and strong. Somewhere else, another picked up the song, then another. Hina told me afterwards that it is an ancient song of sorrow, a song for the loss of a lover. About twenty or thirty people joined them at the next verse, then more and more until the whole square, the night, filled with the singing. The particular tone of one of the women nearby reached me and I found myself crying, gentle tears on my cheeks. The soldiers stood motionless and the Armage conferred with one of the guards. The captive woman started moving to and fro, shifting from one foot to the other, seemingly to the rhythm of the singing. A single human, the focus of all.

I had asked Mylia about the place of the individual, only three days previously:

'There's no such thing. None. Except in a very special sense. One human is not a sufficiently complex system. A person alone is nothing, worthless, can't survive, can't reproduce. There have been instances, here and there, of children found in the wild, of children reared by animals. I've read accounts, old stories.'

'This has also happened on Earth, long ago. There was a king who was said to have had a child brought up among cattle, denied all human contact. To satisfy his curiosity.'

Mylia nodded and looked down, drew a circle on the earth with her foot. She said: 'These children, they have no mind, as we would understand it. No spirit. The mind is a special complexity, held and guarded by society, like language. Your individuals die, but the mind continues, speech continues. The will, the ability to love, to cherish life, these are held and passed on by the communion of humans.'

'Is the, er, single person, unable to change things, unable to change this, whatever you call it, society?'

'Everything changes, the matrices are born new all the time. For a change to be real, to have energy, fire and meaning, it must change not only its society, but also the way that things are passed on, are reproduced. Such a change is also a communion.'

I thought I'd caught her out, for once: 'And where do new things, new ideas come from then?'

'From the womb of the mother and the seed of the father, from combinations and what may look like chance events in the body of the human matrix and the way it relates to the substrate. Societies are not static things, and new ideas that can breed and perpetuate themselves can be incorporated: are, all the time. Even this idea of an individual, of a separate self, lives only in the body of the

mother. And don't forget how easily this isolated being can stray from the path of equality.'

A single being now, out there, swaying in the song. And then without warning something happens to her. I do not know the proper words for it. Battle-frenzy, perhaps, berserker rage, I don't know. It was the first and only time that I ever saw a student of weapons from Imbr-ast in action.

In a single smooth movement, she took a guard's weapon from him and put an energy beam through his legs. He screamed and fell, and the other troops turned. The thing which was for me the strangest was that the singing continued, and the tears carried on down my cheeks. She moved, a flicker of fire. I could see clearly the fine bluish beam from her weapon, piercing the nearest vehicle, and there was an explosion of fuel. People started running and shouting. Mylia came to me, still singing, and held my hand. By the time I looked back, the woman was dead, smoke coming from her clothes. The armoured car burned and the soldiers milled around like ants.

The troops stayed two days. Kinten appeared only once, with his arm in a sling. I kept out of their way, not wanting to draw attention to myself. The people were always polite and tolerant towards them, as in the library. But they behaved like dumb villagers, ignorant of anything.

Mylia found me in my room. 'I spoke to the great Kinten.' She strutted in imitation of his armoured walk. 'I asked him for permission to burn Nahir. He asked me who I was, and I said I was her cousin. I have never before had to ask for permission to burn the dead.'

The phone rings. *Save onto diskette, get up, go to answer....*

It's Aatjie!

— You'll have to speak up, the line's lousy. I can hardly

hear you. Wait. Let me dial nought. Hello. Is that better?
Hello?

— Hello Billy.

*Speak before he can say anything, before he can even give
his name.*

— What's your number there? Can't talk now, I'll phone
you back. Ten minutes, okay? Wait, let me get a pen.

*Now where's the pen? Over to the desk, shit, run through to
the bedroom, look in the jacket. Not here. Downstairs, there's
one in the kitchen on the fridge thingie. Phone's probably
tapped, cue and review, all those tapes spinning in some government office, hooked into some massive mainframe system.*

— Hang on, I've just got to go downstairs for the pen.
Won't be a mo.

He comes back up with the fridge pen, dangling a
bouncy spiral cord and plastic sucker.

— Okay, what's the number there? Double-six three oh
nine one. Right. Speak to you in ten minutes. Cheers.

Billy puts on his raincoat taking its stiffish scarecrow
shape from the hook behind the door, gets the umbrella
and walks out, down to the corner café. It's a small shop,
with all the sweets, smells, a fridge for Cokes. Three kids
crowd around a video-game machine: the sound of Aliens
being taken out.

He stamps his feet, shakes out the umbrella. In the
corner is a red pay-phone, with cigarette burns on its little
table. He fumbles in the raincoat pocket for the number
which is written on the back of a brown envelope, folded.
Here. Dial, wait for the ringing tone.

— Joemat, hullo.

— Uh, hi. Can I speak to Fuad, please?

— Jus' hang on.

He hears music in the background. A voice shouts,
'Aatjie!'

— Hello, is that you Billy?

— Ja. Sorry to keep you. I, er is it okay to talk?

— No, fine. Listen, can you meet me in town on the ninth? That's a Wednesday. At Greenmarket Square, one o'clock. Say, on the corner of Burg and Longmarket?

— Oh, sure. Should I bring anything? You know, just in *case?*

— Ja. That's what I was going to say.

— Listen, are you all right?

— I'm all right ou Billy, man. Don't worry about me. Really. And you?

— I'm, I'm well. You and Farieda must come around for a meal. Still got my number, haven't you?

— Ja. I'll phone you. See you next Wednesday then. One o'clock.

— Sure. Take care, hey.

— You too, stay well.

And the line goes dead.

... we'll have lunch together, and I'll ask him, he'll know. Maybe, yes, he'll take me with him.

This is a world where he can lose himself. The real one can't come in here: a world of whispered conspiracy, of shifting documents, of names, meetings in the night. This is the world of the briefcase, of slipping over borders, swimming the river, code names, hidden comrades.

Like the acid days, only more — what? — yes, mature, more serious. Where actions have precise consequences, where I can live by my wits, with Aatjie and Farieda and, and.... Cars in the night, slipping past the roadblocks with the stuff packed in, where? In the tyres, in the roof lining. A white courier, I could be a courier, wear my business suit, the grey three-piece, and look so urbane and cool that nobody, not the whoever they are.... Drive a smooth car, they'd never pick on a BMW or a Merc. I could show them a thing or two about how to do it. And fiddling with computer things for them. Accessing the databanks, hacking my way into the countrywide security networks, ja, a little tap laid next to the dedicated line, hmm, amplifier two chips and a penlight battery, modem.... Aatjie's the ace, the key for me.

Home again, keys, oh shit locked out.

Magnifying Mirror

6 July 1986

She's moved in, a week ago. He helped her, carrying boxes, carrying furniture, loading the old fridge onto the borrowed van to take it down to the second-hand store. And each new thing, each object with its particular history as it's added to the load, feels like another oppression. Her clothes in his cupboard, her cosmetics in his bathroom. Her ornaments in all the rooms, paintings, a pencil and water-colour drawing from the time when artists, in the Cape anyway, were drawing bones, birds' skulls, skeletons.

He's been eating off unfamiliar plates, eating food prepared slightly differently, even using precisely the same ingredients. Tonight she's off at a meeting, Black Sash, whatever. For the last while, since that weekend at Onrust, she's been at meetings, meetings, meetings, and at the Red Cross doing relief work. But never saying anything about it, never trying to tell him, waiting for him to ask. So that it's become a point of pride with him, his donkey streak, not to ask, to reflect her discreet silence with a disgruntled one. She's been trying to talk other things out though and he's been on the defensive, telling her — Yes it's fine. No, I'm just in a bad mood over something at work.

Though there are times, lying in bed late and looking at her, strange curtain shadows on the wall from the street-light outside, when he can feel an almost painful sweetness of love cutting up from his belly and into his throat. She's calmly there, herself.

He's stopped reading the papers now, telling her that it's because of the book, telling himself too. And the TV's gone. On the day of the move, they'd looked at their two identical Sony Portables and decided that both must go. Tensions in the land mount, invisible on the table where the set used to stand.

He feels the book growing in him. Two diskettes now, apart from backups.

That's, let's see ... 362496 bytes per diskette at an average of say, six bytes per word, makes about sixty thousand, that's a hundred, hundred and twenty thousand words. Of which at least half are notes. And a lot of the rest needs cutting.

But tonight nothing's happening. He's pacing, pacing.

Got the first little barb worked out, bugger up the backups one by one. Write fake data, spike the logs. That should take, um, rollover of three months. Nobody re-reads backup data, and if the change's made on a bit-pattern level they'll never unscramble it. Same amount of data goes onto the tapes and off into the fireproof room somewhere. Return a message: VERIFY BACKUP PROCEDURE COMPLETED AND LOGGED. *I can fuck up the drives with a supertight read-write loop that slips in past the operating system, wham whamming the iskheads up and down till the whole thing just stops. Hardware failure. But erase the procedures from storage as they come online, in case. They must never suspect, what if they suspect now?*

He gets a pencil, starts scrawling on the wirebound stenographer's pad that they use for shopping-lists. Notes.

In Assembler Language, run this through a little program to turn it into Binary. I should be able to write that in two or three lunchbreaks at work. Who the hell reads Binary these days, when everything's fourth-generation and spread-sheets?

A car outside, he goes to the window, parts the curtains

an inch with one finger and peers out. Sue. When she gets in, he's sitting on the beige carpet with the pad.

— Hi. Nice meeting?

— Mm-mm. What've you been up to?

— Oh, work stuff. A little catching up.

He waves a hand at the notes. She doesn't even look, comes over to kiss him. Then into the kitchen to put the kettle on.

— Tea?

— Mmm. Rooibos if you're making.

— Anything new on the book?

— Not tonight.

— What's the matter? Are you in a bad mood?

— No.

— What is it then? You're behaving like a statue. Old Boniface.

He stands up and goes rigid like the statue of Rhodes in the Botanical Gardens. Right hand raised in a Hitler salute, *White Man, your Hinterland lies yonder*. She puts the teacups down and stands looking at him. His face is held hard, his eyes stare out, towards the picture above the fireplace. She says:

— Look at *Il Duce* himself.

— Are you accusing me of being a Fascist? Is that it? You get so fucking self-righteous.

— I'm not accusing you of anything.

— But you are. I feel accused all the time. By your meetings, by, well, just by you. You're so bloody *right*, so correct. It presses down on me.

— Well, if me being a member of the Sash feels correct, why don't you do something. Join, make a statement.

— The Black Sash happens to be a women's organisation. Which is to say a sort of inverse sexism.

— Ooh, listen to it! Who's being a purist now? You couldn't even join the Boy Scouts. Do you want to know something? I think you're a closet radical, a Marxist even.

And you spend all your time shoring up the walls of that closet from the inside. Another beam here, another sheet of iron there, a few more studs and bolts and nails. Because if you ever came out, you'd feel like you were having one of those horrible dreams when you're naked in a public place. You'd have to act, to do something.

— Yes, I am a closet Marxist, but with a K. Me! I'm a closet me! I don't need to find *my* identity by sinking in some great swamp of a mass movement.

— You don't need to find your identity, period. Because all you'd find is a great big sagging sphincter. A *slapgat*. What's your woman in the book saying to you? Did you ever ask her what she'd do here? Now? No, of course not. 'She's got her own identity, *she* only says what she wants to.' Who is she? Where does she come from?

— Ooh, such sly discourse! Did you do rhetoric in first year? Hear the great woman speak.

— You pig. Who was this Monsieur Chauvin, that you should be named after him? Was there a Monsieur Bigot, too? You'd have got on famously with them.

— That's great, just fantastic. I have to stand here in my own house and listen to you insulting me. Mock on, mock on, I don't give a shit!

— The cornered weasel hissing and snapping from fear. Wait, I want to show you something.

And she turns and heads up to the bedroom. Extra-heavy tread on the stairs for emphasis. When she comes down again she's holding the make-up mirror, the magnifying one. He stands up and comes to her, tries to put his arm around her waist.

— Put it away. I don't want to fight. Really.

— And nor do I. But just take one little look. William Marks.

All huge and distorted, with pores in his nose. One big roadmap veined eye, blinking. The image wobbles in her shaking hand.

— What did you mean by a closet Marxist?

— Go and read your book. Have you read *Capital*?

— Bits, and the *For Beginners*.

— That thing that she says about work, how does it go? All value comes from work or something. A bit suspiciously like the Labour Theory, don't you think?

— Ah, shit. It's different, totally different. She gets the idea from biology, from her crazy systems theories. Not from economics. I don't even think that she'd understand politics, as we use the word. And it's *just a book*. How often do I have to say that before it sinks into your tiny little mind?

— Just a book! You're letting your bloody life be just a book. And I *just* happen to live here. And the country is *just* a wounded animal bleeding into the ground. Just a this, just a that, and you never fucking take anything in your hand, make it real.

She grabs his nose and twists, — See, not just a nose, a real one! You and your metaphors. If you ever followed one to the end, you might get a little shock. I'm going to bed.

He stands in the study. Papers in neat piles, papers with red pen scrawling, with machine perfect daisywheel typing, papers, bits of the book.

' ... we have no property here, no damming up of the fires of life in one part of the web. Our ideas will not accommodate it. If consciousness locates itself towards tyranny or submission, then society's ideas must be acting to define that position as normal. If these have, and those are without, there must be some way of thinking telling us that this is correct. A teaching that perpetuates itself.'

and

'The accumulation of energy into property creates a thing called an economy. A system of equivalences arises in the body of society, which can be used to represent these values. This is called money. Money equates things

*and processes that have no connection except as mediated
by consciousness. A study of economy must start by under-
standing the process by which the mind creates corespon-
dences between disparate things. We must understand that
these connections are in consciousness and not in reality,
not in the matrices. The hawk does not buy the field-
mouse.'*

He turns the light on, stands in the bedroom doorway.

— Sue.

— Hm.

— I want to tell you something.

She lifts herself onto her elbow, looks at him with
screwed-up eyes.

— When I was twenty-one, when I was still a hippy,
something happened to me. I find it very difficult to talk
about.

He comes to sit on the end of the bed. Outside it is
raining again, and he can hear the leak dripping tic tic on
the landing. His feet are cold, in blue stretch-towelling
socks.

— I lived in a big old house in New Church Street,
above Town. In a commune, with a whole bunch of other
people. Freaks, heads, we were stoned the whole time. We
thought the world was going to be completely rebuilt, you
know, that there'd be a new consciousness or something. It
was very vague, very stoned, but it felt so, how can I say,
so real. You smoked something, or ate something, and the
... the world actually changed. Like Alice. This must all
sound very stupid.

— No. Well, yes. But I understand.

— There was this woman, it was really her house. Jessica Winter. She taught psychology. You may remember,
there was a big fuss about it at the time. In the papers and
everything. She killed herself, slit her wrists. In the bath.
I, uh, I was the person who found her. I mean found her
dead. In the bath. There was blood, blood and water ...

He is shivering now, his hands fluttering. She moves to him, pulls his shaking body against her bare skin. Her fingers in the curls. The low moaning sound of a wounded animal, bleeding internally.

— There was nothing, nothing … I could do. No matter how hard I tried.

Pigeons and Gulls

9 July 1986

It's town, lunchtime. He's standing on Greenmarket Square, holding the briefcase. A preacher is screaming out the Gospel to an audience of two and there are workers on the benches, eating lunch; a sandwich, a bunny chow: half a white loaf with the middle ripped out, stuffed with a can of pilchards. The pigeons are everywhere; a few gulls screech and stagger on the air. A saxophonist with a hat placed hopefully on the cobbles plays a long slow blues, the notes all blurry and slightly drunk in the noon sun. The flea-market is smaller, shrunk by winter or a rotting economy, but the crowds still move through, the bits of old brass and copper set out on the long trestles still reflect.

Mylia, what if she were to come here? And what would she look like here on the square? She comes across from behind those trees, what's she wearing? Trousers, loose ones, hand-woven with a fine interlock pattern, like the tiles of a mosque. And a long loose top. Boots, the hard felt ones with embroidery and wooden soles.

Here she's only a crazy old woman, an eccentric. Pigeons, she's never seen pigeons before. She goes and squats near them there, where they're eating that soggy white bread on the cobbles. Who squats? Nobody. Seven minutes to go. And she'd just look at the birds, from close by. They come right up to your hand. Flash! she's got one, the wings pumping help-lessly against her fingers. She turns it upside-down, and care-

fully starts to unpick the threads that are wound around the red feet, cutting into the flesh. Hell, half the pigeons in town must be crippled with pieces of thread, cotton, nylon. Maybe they use them for building nests. Nobody'd look at her; nobody pays attention to crazy old women.

Three blue-uniform policemen walk towards him, he checks his watch, looks at the clock above the hotel. His knuckles are pale and his palm feels slippery from gripping the briefcase handle. He takes his weight on the right foot, on the left, the policemen pass, heading on towards the Cape Times building. Down where the delivery people are loading neat new-printed heaps of the *Argus* into vans. Four minutes ... He shifts the case into the right hand now.

He'll come from over the square, up from Shortmarket Street. With his jaunty walk, a sort of joller's strut. Ducking under those trees, up past the row of ... they look like an avenue of lingams, over the cobbles. He'll signal below his waist with his hand, little finger and index finger out, safe. How do you blow up a safe? How do you blow up a system? But a system's got the seeds of its own explosion in it, you just have to program it right, intercept with interrupts in under past the operating software, just let the force of some of those little built-in routines come out and —, shit, one minute to go. Is he up on the hotel veranda, watching me? I'd watch me for a good ten, twenty minutes, check out all the angles, look for him. A face in a window, up there. Not him. On the roof, way up on Kimberley House? No.

I won't say anything, won't hand over straight away, just fall into step with him and we'll walk over to ... to the Gardens, to a fast-food place down in the underground Mall, he's late. Late, I'd be late, checking out the angles. Then we can talk, he owes it to me. How long now, two months? One minute late. What if the Crencor bunch have got me covered too? Those guys on the bench over there, they could be ...

A Volvo pulls up next to him, hoots. He bends down,

peers into the car. Four men. The driver has mirror
shades, looks strong and heavy with rolled-up sleeves,
biceps, a tattoo. The back door opens:

*Yes, it's him! But he's shaved his beard, hell, hardly recog-
nised him.*

Aatjie beckons, silent and urgent, and Billy trots over to
the car. The others ignore him, the driver, cool, taciturn,
scans up and down the square.

He takes the case — Thanks, man — and flips it onto
the other back-seat passenger's lap. The car pulls away,
down Longmarket, gone. The preacher's voice and the
saxophone wail over the square.

A High Wooden House

Faced with the alternatives of arresting the entire community or leaving, the troops have gone, roaring out over the fields, taking their dead. The people's calm and stubborn refusal to acknowledge them has puzzled and, temporarily at least, conquered them. I think of Kinten as a dog that rushed out to bark, and found no thief but its own master.

Down in the big square, a wooden structure has been built, a loose house, with timbers piled over each other. A pyre for Nahir. It is night and the moons are both up again, the moons with their rich and complicated mythology. The people have gathered in a great circle, dressed in their finest clothes. They carry lights, torches of fire, and the flame shines on the bright colours of the cloth, red and orange, ochre, blue. Someone is bowing a stringed instrument, big and deep, sounding a bit like a cello or a man's voice. A cadenced drum speaks.

Towards one side the crowd stirs. The circle parts and they come bearing her naked body on a pallet, high over their heads. There are ten or fifteen people with their arms raised, holding the poles, and Mylia is one of them, third from the front on the right. The body shines with oil, shines in the torchlight. I think I can see her death-wounds, dark on her side. The circle closes.

Using the long poles, they place the body on the pyre, slowly lowering it onto the top. Four youths climb up and *complete the structure so that it closes over her, laying long new planks in a crossover pattern. The bowed music and the drum stop and the bearers move back to the circle. There is a long silence. Two men walk towards the structure and throw their torches into the hollow at the base, then return to their places. Her brothers. Their walk is slow and dignified and they link arms on the way back. Three or four more come with their flames, return. The house of the dead is burning now. And for half an hour or more, people walk out towards the pyre and add their brands. When I feel that it is my turn, I too take my small piece of flame to the great one. The fire is so hot now that I have to hurl the brand. It moves like a comet to join the others.*

There is silence and the roaring and bursting of the pyre. The people stand facing in and after a while join hands to form three great concentric circles. I feel a rough old man's calloused skin, and the tender hand of a child. A woman's voice starts to chant a high screaming dirge, on and on, and then all the voices reply, all the breath in living throats. A song of the flame piercing and living into the night, louder and fuller. The circles begin to sway, slowly at first, left and right. The chant and the reply.

The whole crowd rocks into and out of itself, fine human bodies in bright clothes. Hands come undone. I see faces in the light of the flames, faces full of joy and fire, singing. Wilder and faster, and there are instruments now, gongs and drums, long sounding horns. On into the night, as the fire lowers and dies away, the dancers move round and round, round and round.